There was chaos and pandemonium and, most of all, fear.

The shotgun blast exploded the lunch counter beside Harry and to his right into thousands of shattered pieces.

Harry held his fire. He had to be careful. The anarchy of the scrambling, terrified people cut low his return-fire potential. He knew the lookout would reload immediately. That meant some leeway. A couple of seconds at least. So Harry ignored him and leaned in front of the blasted section of counter.

As he did, the area directly behind him, a pie case and mirror, blew apart as several cross-fired slugs ripped into it. Slivers of glass and chips of plates sprayed out in every direction.

Harry spun, crouched low, and fired at the leader. The bullet caught the would-be robber chest high, whirled him around, and whacked him over a table.

Another double-barreled blast splintered the counter on Harry's other side. This one was close, he noted. Too damned close.

Harry popped a shot at the lookout and splattered his throat. The punch of the bullets slammed the shotgun man back against the wall, where he slid, quite slowly, to the floor and gurgled away his life in great red gobs.

Harry was anticipating a clear shot at one of the other punks when he heard the sound of pistol fire and felt a surge of hot air blow by his head.

He spun to see the staggering, bleeding leader aiming at him for another try . . .

SUDDEN IMPACT

by Joseph C. Stinson

Screenplay by Joseph C. Stinson
Story by Earl E. Smith & Charles B. Pierce

WARNER BOOKS

A Warner Communications Company

Warner Books, Inc.,
666 Fifth Avenue,
New York, N.Y. 10103

 A Warner-Communications Company

Printed in the United States of America

First Warner Books Printing: *December, 1983*

10 9 8 7 6 5 4 3 2 1

SUDDEN IMPACT

1

The city.

San Francisco.

Surrounded on three sides by ocean and bay and their joining together.

It rests now, lulled asleep by the ebb and flow of water lapping and whooshing against its edges. Softly. Quietly. Endlessly.

Swathed in darkness, calmed by night. It recharges.

With the coming of the dawning sun, it will rise as it has risen every other morning of its past. To grow. To prosper. To reward. To punish. To spread joy. To inflict pain. To attack. To be attacked. To extend its life. To approach its death.

But on this night, as on all the other nights of its history, it regroups. Its wounds heal, its ambitions breed, its passions foment.

It regenerates itself.

Fog, delicate and serpentine, billows in from the sea and

masks the city and its proud monuments in damp, chilly gray. It envelops bridges, towers, and skyscrapers. It caresses their defiant upreach and shrouds them in glistening mist.

At the city's western edge, the fog, in its fullest, thickest motion, gently encircles the Esplanade and Great Highway. It wraps itself around the Seal Rocks, which are empty of their sunning, barking, blubbery daytime bodies. It creeps along Ocean Beach, which is, except for the constant dying of waves on its sand, silent and still. It enfolds the Cliff House, which perches vulnerably between sea and sky, waiting for the energy, fun, and profit of day and people.

The gray coils around the single car in the restaurant's parking lot. A long black not-so-new Cadillac.

The car collects the moisture of the fog and beads it into drops that run downward over bumps and dents and grime to trickle slowly to the ground.

The car's personalized license plates read SILKY. The windows are nearly opaque with wetness. Through the windshield two shadows can be just barely discerned.

One shadow is a man.

He is large and, though clearly not old, his round, pulpy features obscure his age. He is perhaps in his mid-twenties. Or thirties. Or forties. His clothes are a garish, multilayered combination of plaids and stripes and bright, conflicting colors. On his head sits a dead rat shaped like a toupé. Or a toupé shaped like a dead rat. On his face sits a wide, one-sided, spread-lipped smirk.

A fleshy, flashy, polyester wonder.

Maneuvering his ample belly and buttocks from under the steering wheel, he slides to his right, toward the other shadow.

A woman.

She looks straight ahead, out through the misty windshield, at the swirling fog.

She wears a gray Burberry trench coat belted at her waist. The coat hugs her slim body. One flap of its skirt is turned over on itself to reveal a triangle of her muted-blue silk dress. Her knees peek out from under her dress hem. She wears navy-blue calfskin high-heeled sandals on her small feet. Her toenails are unpainted.

The cloying scent of overly applied discount-drugstore cologne fills her nostrils. Yet it fails to conceal the briny odor of perspiration that prickles her nose.

She turns her head toward her sliding companion as he approaches her. He is breathing heavily now.

She wonders, Effort or anticipation?

Her hair is soft and fine. It is parted on the side and fans out to frame her face in blondness. The face itself is small; the skin is smooth and very white. Her features are slightly angular, her chin strong. Her eyes are blue and ovaled by long nearly white lashes. Her lips are full and pink, though she wears no lipstick.

A navy-blue canvas shoulder bag is looped around her left shoulder. She clamps it under her elbow, close to her body.

As he comes close she tenses.

The bag is between them.

As he hooks a beefy arm around her neck she flinches.

He relaxes his smirk to purse his lips and coo at her. "Take it easy, baby. Cool yourself out. You're in good hands."

His fat, knuckly fingers fondle her cheek.

Her own hands, gloved in soft navy-blue leather, are clenched into tight fists.

She stares at his circle face.

It is flushed a blotchy red and shines under a patina of sweat.

As he moves his left arm she presses her knees tightly together. Her kneecaps drain white from the force.

He notices and makes more cooing sounds.

"Hey, baby, don't be so uptight. You're gonna have a sweet time tonight."

She does not respond.

"You wanna pop a stick? I got great stuff. Primo, babe. It'll cool you out nice."

She shakes her head. No.

"How about a little taste, then? Got a pint of apricot brandy under the seat. No glasses, so you'll have to swig, but what the hell."

She shakes her head again. No.

"Hey, you're organic, huh? You like it *au naturel*." He chuckles. "Me, too. But I like it any old goddamned way I can get it." He chuckles some more. His girth heaves up with each wheezy intake of breath.

She stares at his upper lip. Beads of sweat have formed there. Big beads, tiny beads, beads of all sizes.

"How about some tunes? Shit, that's organic, ain't it? I got one that'll work for you. Never fuckin' fails."

He reaches across her.

She does not flinch at his movement. She focuses on his lip and on all the little beads.

He pops open the glove box and yanks out a cassette. He knocks the compartment closed and jams the cassette into the car's stereo.

"Wait'll you hear this system, babe. You'll cream your drawers." He chuckles snidely. "Yeah, you're gonna love it." He draws out the word "love," rasping it deep in his throat, and stretches it into two syllables.

He flicks on the stereo, adjusts its level and balance and tone as music plays.

At the first flash of sound, she looks away from him and at the machine.

She identifies the music instantly.

The song is "I've Got a Feeling."

First cut. Side two. Beatles.

The *Let It Be* album.

The album with the song.

The song.

With a splayed nicotine-stained index finger, he pushes the fast-forward button.

She looks back at him. At his entire face.

Dear God, she thinks, he's not searching for the song? He's not going to play that song? The same song?

He lifts his finger from the switch.

No sound comes from the stereo.

"I nail it every time," he says with pride.

He sinks backward in the car seat.

"Now, honey, just lay back and let it be." He elongates the "be." Rasps it.

A song begins.

A voice. McCartney. Notes on a piano.

"The long and winding road . . ."

The song.

Orchestration.

"That leads to your door
Will never disappear . . ."

He's playing it, she thinks. He really is. So be it.

She looks out at the fog.

His right arm, which till now had been hanging loosely

around her neck, starts to slide slowly over her shoulder and down, around, then under her arm.

She feels his fingers plying her side, searching for a hold on her breast.

She is grateful for the durable fabric of her trench coat.

His left hand moves to her knee, grasps it, then slides slowly up and along the inside of her leg.

She is glad for the thin intervention of stocking between her skin and his.

> *"The wild and windy night*
> *That the rain washed away*
> *Has left me full of tears*
> *Crying for the day . . ."*

As the hand travels along her thigh she relaxes her right fist and moves her hand toward him.

She reaches to his crotch.

Then, without touching him and still looking at his face, she finds his zipper and slowly pulls it downward.

The actions of both his hands stop.

He nestles backward and smiles a wide yellow-toothed smile.

As his fly widens with the unzipping, his paunch, unrestrained, spills out.

> *"Many times I've been alone*
> *And many times I've cried . . ."*

When his fly is fully open, he breathily pleads. "Yeah, baby . . . oh, baby . . ."

She draws her hand back, releases her hold on her shoulder bag, and softly, deftly, reaches into it.

His head lolls back now, his eyes close, and his moaned entreaties become almost whimpers.

"Anyway you'll never know
The many ways I've tried..."

She withdraws her hand from her bag.
In it she holds a shiny, silvery .38-caliber Colt revolver.

"And still they lead me back
To the long winding road..."

She glides the gun to his crotch and slowly, gingerly slides its barrel into his open fly.
He flinches at its touch, then relaxes and moans appreciatively, "Oh, yeah, baby..."

"And still they lead me back
To the long, winding road
You left me standing here
A long, long time ago..."

She cocks the hammer of the pistol.
His eyes open.
His head bobs upright.

The fog curls itself around the Cadillac, entwining the car in airy spirals of gray.
There is a muffled boom within the car. Then another.
Then, except for water sounds, silence.
The passenger door of the car bursts open.
The fog slithers in and fills the car.
Small feet in high-heeled sandals touch the ground.

The woman steps from the car and walks to the cliff wall. The clicking of her heels is neither slow nor fast.

Standing at the cliff edge, she looks out to sea. Her eyes are clear. Her face is placid.

She lifts her left hand. It holds a cassette. She flings it out into the water below.

She lifts her other hand. It holds the gun.

The barrel is tipped with blood.

She stares at the wet redness.

After a moment she stoops, grabs a scrap of newspaper litter, and wipes the gun barrel clean. She crumples the paper and tosses it over the cliff. She watches it bounce down the rocks into the water below. She follows its progress as it rises on a swell and floats away.

She replaces the gun in her bag, then looks back at the Cadillac.

Her eyes are different now.

They burn.

Abruptly she turns and walks off, into the gray.

2

Although it was only five minutes to nine, Anthony J. D'Ambrosia was already having a bad day.

No one in the courtroom would have guessed by looking at him that the dark, fortyish, mustachioed assistant district attorney had slept through his alarm, missing his morning three-mile run, hurried through his shower and shave, skipped his high-fiber breakfast, and forgotten to restock his briefcase with herbal tea bags. But here he was, sitting calmly in his prosecutor's chair and wondering whether to run tonight or to double his distance tomorrow. And he was rubbing his chin to see if the three gashes he'd given himself with a dull razor and a nervous hand had stopped bleeding. He was also fervently hoping that his stomach wouldn't start growling from hunger while, at the same time, he was doing his best to resist a king-size caffeine craving.

Yet, nonetheless, he knew that all these problems combined would be nothing compared to the trouble he'd face if

Callahan were late to, even worse—much worse—absent from this arraignment hearing.

He checked his jogger's digital wristwatch. Three minutes to nine. Callahan hated court appearances and always cut them close, but this was too damned close. And with Judge Lundstrom on the beach today . . .

D'Ambrosia sat up in his chair. His stomach was growling. Shit. He stood, cleared his throat loudly to cover the rumblings, adjusted his vest and tie, and paced behind his chair. He eyed the wall clock at the rear of the courtroom.

The double doors below the large Roman-numeraled time-piece were still closed.

Two minutes to nine.

Where the hell was Callahan?

He looked over at the defendant's table. Dave Mahaffey was a competent lawyer and a decent man, but his sense of client selectivity was clearly deteriorating. Hawkins was a contemporary illustration of an old penal cliché—the incorrigible criminal. In modern sociolegalese, he was a recidivist. Which simply meant he didn't give a damn. His "tendency to relapse into previous criminal behavior" could be translated to "He's got nothing to lose because he knows he can beat the rap." The budding Little Caesar was barely twenty-three, but his record was perversely impressive. Seventeen arrests. All for crimes of violence. Zero convictions. Witnesses against him seemed to have a strange way of changing testimony or reneging on original identifications. Hawkins had breezed through his series of arrests, arraignments, and trials with the shrewd, expert assistance of Sinclair Turner, a portly, elderly, thoroughly corrupt veteran of the judiciary wars. But Turner had recently retired, the victim of a slow bladder, a lazy colon, an arrhythmic heart, and the close, unwelcome scrutiny of the bar association's ethics committee.

Poor Hawkins, D'Ambrosia thought as he sat down. He'd soon find that Dave Mahaffey was no Sinclair Turner. Thank God. For Mahaffey's sake.

He checked the clock on the back wall.

One minute to nine.

Goddamned Callahan.

D'Ambrosia grumbled a litany of imaginatively obscene epithets to himself and leaned back. Maybe Hawkins wouldn't need anyone. The evidence was thin, to be sure. He'd much rather have gone in stronger, but he had no choice. It was now or never. He couldn't wait any longer. This one was clearly a cross-your-fingers, get-the-indictment, and scramble-like-hell-till-trial-time deal.

But if Callahan, the arresting officer, didn't show, then both he and Harry could bend over and kiss their asses good-bye. And wouldn't Harry the hard case love that.

D'Ambrosia gave the back doors one last, hopeful glance. Nothing. The bastard. That arrogant, self-satisfied son of a—

The somber tone of the bailiff interrupted his silent diatribe. D'Ambrosia stood and faced the front of the court.

"... Court of the State of California is now in session. The Honorable Judge Lundstrom presiding."

D'Ambrosia felt his ears heat up. He hoped like hell they were not turning red. His new, shorter hairstyle offered no camouflage.

The judge stepped deliberately to the bench and sat behind the imposing block of polished blond wood. The bailiff sounded a staid "Please be seated" and ceremoniously walked across the courtroom to sit at his station.

Here it comes, thought D'Ambrosia as he and everyone else in the room sat down. Here it comes and right at me. He watched the judge open the appropriate file, look it over briefly, peer over at Hawkins and then at him.

He tried not to squirm.

The judge was about to speak but instead looked up, surprised and visibly perturbed, to the rear of the courtroom.

D'Ambrosia turned and looked, too. He saw a tall, lean, very fit man striding up the center aisle while removing a pair of dark wraparound sunglasses. Inspector Harry Callahan. San Francisco Police Department. A cocky, tough-assed, insufferable son of a bitch. But a damn good cop. Maybe the best in the city.

Callahan slid the sunglasses into the inside breast pocket of his brown herringbone sport jacket, adjusted his dark brown tie, and sat down behind D'Ambrosia, who shook his head wearily at him and turned back to face the judge.

Lundstrom was glaring. Steel-gray hair, close cropped and brushed back. Neat but loose, not sprayed. A long, rather narrow face, lined by age and experience but still soft at the cheeks. Hazel eyes, a sharp nose, and brilliantly white teeth.

Not a bad-looking woman, considering her age, D'Ambrosia thought. But one hell of an ice maiden. And a real Callahan fan.

He did not have to turn around to know that Harry was glaring back at the judge. Nothing beats a little touch of humble tact. Harry was just terrific at winning the easy points.

Lundstrom broke her stare and spoke in an elegantly stern tone.

"Mr. D'Ambrosia, this case is a travesty."

Oh, Christ.

"You have no evidence whatsoever linking the accused to the murder. The gun found in his car was obtained as the result of an illegal search. In the eyes of the Court it does not exist.''

God damn. He knew it was a long shot but, shit, she was coming down hard.

''The search was illegal because Inspector Callahan''—she paused and smiled an icy smile—''and this is an old story, did not have sufficient probable cause for detaining Mr. Hawkins. The gun is inadmissible and the charges against the defendant are therefore dismissed.'' She closed the file slowly.

D'Ambrosia grabbed a pencil and twisted it in his fingers. She was not finished, however.

''Mr. D'Ambrosia, be assured I will discuss your case-preparation techniques with the district attorney. Bailiff, next.''

D'Ambrosia gaped. The pencil broke. He flipped open his briefcase, tossed the pieces inside, scooped up his papers, threw them aside, too, slammed the case shut, rose from his chair, turned on his heel, and stormed out of the courtroom.

He did not look at Callahan.

Harry sagged in his chair.

He was tired.

He'd worked too long on too many bullshit dead-end cases the night before. Or was it this morning? Didn't really matter anymore. The days were blending into nights, the nights into days, forming a perfectly straight gray line of frustration.

And now this. He'd come all the way the hell down here to be slapped on the wrist like some schoolboy caught with his hands in his pockets. By a prissy knee-jerk judge who pictured herself the model for the statue of the lady with the blindfold and the scales. But that didn't matter, either. What mattered was that a scum like Hawkins had walked again.

How had everything got so screwed up?

Or was he kidding himself? Was it a trick of his memory

that made the bad old days seem so much better than the lousy new ones?

Maybe it was just a sign of getting . . . tired.

Harry almost laughed to himself but stopped when he noticed a more vocal, raucous mirth on the other side of the courtroom.

Hawkins and his pals were congratulating one another.

Harry watched them. He knew what was coming. The faces change, but slime ways always stay the same. He could get up and leave, but why spoil the ritual? After all, you got to respect some traditions. Besides, it would make the next move—his move—and he knew it would come, inevitably, sometime, somewhere—all the more sweet. So he sat his ground and watched. And waited.

Hawkins and his two cronies smirked and sniggered and smacked high fives.

Lundstrom shot a glance their way.

Harry wondered what would happen if they kept it up. Maybe if they got real naughty, she'd make them clap erasers after court or write on the blackboard a thousand times, "I must not make a mockery of the justice system and laugh about it out loud in court."

Hawkins and his friends finally broke it up and started to leave. They walked to the center aisle and turned toward the rear of the room.

There, right on the aisle, sat Harry.

Hawkins had spiffed himself up nice for court. He'd washed the pomaded spiked hairdo away, cold-creamed the red swastikas and lightning bolts off his cheeks, and removed his safety-pin earring. Now he looked just like any other Waspy blond American young man on the way up in his chosen profession. His pals, however, had seen no need to dress up, so they'd come in their work clothes. Straight from the factory, so to speak. Plenty of leather and zippers and chains and spikes and all the rest of the required scum wear. The faces may change, but slime ways always remain the same.

Hawkins and his two friends halted in the middle of the aisle when they saw Callahan.

They stood absolutely still and totally expressionless as they stared at Harry.

Harry stared back.

Slowly Hawkins's face slid into a grin. The cronies followed his lead. The grins led to giggling and Hawkins extended an open hand, palm up, to each of his pals. They slapped his palms loudly with their own and sway-assed their best scum strut out of the room.

Harry did not watch them go.

He rose from his chair and left the courtroom.

He'd remember.

Harry entered the courthouse corridor and made straight for the elevator. Hawkins and his pals were nowhere to be seen. Harry knew that they were in the men's lavatory. He also knew what they were doing there. Laying some lines and rolling some bills. He knew that if he chose to, he could nail their asses good-bye just by walking into that men's room. But the hell with that. He was no narc. He'd nail the bastards but not for sniffing some goddamned nose candy. He was a homicide cop. A damned good one. Best in the goddamned city, to his mind. Maybe in the whole goddamned country, the whole goddamned world. He caught up with his anger. Yeah, sure. In any event, he'd nail them. And for what they'd done too many times. Murder.

D'Ambrosia and the defense attorney were shaking hands in front of the elevator. As the defense guy walked away

Harry heard them arrange a racquet-ball hour for later that afternoon. Racquet ball. Great.

D'Ambrosia was pressing the down button when Harry reached his side. He gave Harry a quick sideways glance and Harry thought he could hear teeth grinding.

"Preventive dentistry," he said, staring forward at the elevator door.

"What?" D'Ambrosia spat out the word. Harry knew he must be really pissed. Couldn't blame him, though.

"It's what you do to keep your teeth in good shape, so you don't need to go to the dentist so much. It's great for the teeth but lousy for the dentist business. Do you know what the suicide rate for dentists is?"

"What the hell are you talking about, Callahan?"

"Preventive dentistry. It's what grinding your teeth cause you're too pissed to talk ain't."

D'Ambrosia stared at him, then exploded.

"How many times, Callahan? How many goddamned son-of-a-bitchin' times? Sixth sense doesn't count anymore. You can't bust them because you *think* they're dirty. Psychic don't cut it."

D'Ambrosia spun around. His ears were bright red.

The elevator doors opened. Harry let him enter first, then stepped into the elevator. It was already fairly crowded with attaché-case types, male and female. And a few regular citizens, too. They were easy to spot. They were the ones who looked so confused.

As the door started to close, Harry heard a commotion in the corridor. Very quickly it approached the elevator. Just before the door shut, a big-knuckled hand topped by a studded black leather wristlet thrust itself between door and jamb. The elevator reopened fully and Hawkins and his cronies stepped in and sauntered to the rear.

Harry could feel the attaché types and the civilians edge away imperceptibly and he thought he could hear D'Ambrosia's teeth again.

Immediately the slime began to whoop it up.

The faces may change...

Harry waited.

The giggles and the sniggers and the sneers built to the unavoidable crescendo.

Then... Hawkins.

"Hey, Callahan, baby, don't look so puked out. Better luck next time—*fool*."

Harry wasted no time. He spun around and, in one fluid movement, seized Hawkins by his sport-jacket lapels and slammed him against the wall at one side of the small close-packed chamber.

Attachés and civilians threw themselves on one another to dodge out of the way. One woman yelped.

Hawkins's cronies made a move to advance, but Hawkins, trying to regain some lost cool, smirked at Harry and waved them back.

Harry, still gripping the lapels, stepped in close to Hawkins and slid him up the wall. Hawkins was a compact, solid five feet ten, but Harry lifted him easily off his feet. When he had hoisted him up to his own six-feet-four level, Harry went nose to nose with the suddenly unsmirking young man. Harry held him tight and unblinkingly glared at him for a few long seconds.

The elevator was silent.

Hawkins's feet dangled.

Harry finally spoke.

"Listen, punk. You're like a pile of dog shit. And lots of things can happen to dog shit. It can be dried up and blown away by the wind. It can be stepped on and squashed. It can

be scraped off the street with a shovel. So take my advice—
be careful where the dog shits you.''

The doors opened at ground-floor level.

The attaché types and civilians hurriedly emptied out and
then broke clear of the elevator.

Harry let go of the lapels.

A shocked Hawkins dropped to his feet and sidled around
Harry. Flanked by his hushed cronies, he bolted out of the
elevator car.

Once they deemed themselves a safe enough distance from
Harry, they tried to recoup their broken cool by hooting and
giggling. But all the while they made sure to watch their
backs carefully as they strolled out of the courthouse.

Harry watched them go. The faces may—

''Class act, Callahan, real class act.''

D'Ambrosia left the elevator and walked quickly along the
corridor.

The doors were closing. Harry stepped out.

He was alone.

Loosening his tie and unbuttoning his collar, Harry walked to
his car. He slipped on his wraparounds and drove off.

He needed a cup of coffee, black and strong. Maybe a lot
of coffees. And some breakfast. Time to head over to Loretta
Brendol's Acorn Café.

Harry drove east on Grove to Market, then cut over to
Battery. There he turned left and drove to Broadway. Loretta's
was part of an endangered species these days. The mom-and-
pop–owned coffee shop/luncheonette. A place where you
could get good food at a fair price and maybe even a genuine,
noncommercial smile.

Harry drove alone. Because he worked alone. There had
been many partners over the years. The many years. He had

even liked some of them. But there had been too many differences that ran too deep. Methods, morality—whatever. Harry had his own way. And, for him, his own way was the only way. So as far as partners were concerned, it was simply lead, follow, or get the hell out of the way.

And, of course, there was the list. The casualty list for Callahan's partners. The body count. It was high. Certainly higher than he'd ever wanted. But he couldn't seem to do much about it. Things just happened. And, of course, the final irony was that the best ones, the really good ones, the ones he liked, they were gone. Di Georgio, Kate Moore, Felton Perry. Of the good ones, only Chico had gotten out alive. Harry had been sorry, but glad, too, to see him go. Last he'd heard, Chico was teaching high school in the Mission District. For the first few years after, Chico would call to invite Harry to dinner on Sundays or holidays. Harry never went. Chico stopped calling. High-school teacher, Harry thought. Hell, these days that was more dangerous than cop work, and they wouldn't let you carry a piece. Luck to Chico.

Harry cleared his mind of these thoughts and just watched the city and people go by. The outdoor daytime scenes were nice and the city was beautiful. But Harry didn't savor the beauty or the serenity. He was all too familiar with the around-the-corner, down-the-street, back-alley action. And the indoor, downstairs, upstairs, back-room activity. And, of course, the nighttime world. That was his action, his world. His job.

Harry pulled up across the street from Loretta's, parked, and walked over, stopping only to drop a quarter in a *Chronicle* box and pick up a newspaper.

He wasn't really hungry and he had tons of bullshit paperwork to wade through, so he decided to grab one to go.

He entered the coffee shop while scanning the headlines

and made straight for the orders-to-go station. Once there, he stood, flipped to the metro section, and read.

Without waiting for word or gesture, a tall, thin, middle-aged woman detached herself from the cash register and moved to the large metal coffee urn. She reached for a large cardboard cup and quickly shoveled in two heaping spoonfuls of sugar. She then filled the cup to its brim with hot, steamy, dark coffee, capped it, stepped to the takeout counter, and placed the container in front of Harry. Without looking up from the paper—he was now reading the editorials and trying to remember about preventive dentistry—Harry slid a dollar bill across the counter, took the coffee, and started to walk toward the door.

As he left he glanced around the coffee shop.

It was full of customers and very quiet. Everyone was either sipping coffee or juice or water, or they were nibbling and picking at their food. Harry also noted the three young black men, each sitting alone in a different corner of the shop.

He continued on his way out.

Once he'd gotten his unmarked started and into traffic, he pried the plastic lid off the coffee container and sipped.

He grimaced and spat the coffee out the window.

He came to a stop at a red light.

He sipped again. Grimaced again. Spat again.

He removed his sunglasses.

As the light changed green Harry capped the coffee, placed it next to him on the seat, and gunned a tight U turn through the intersection, ignoring the horns and shouts of angry fellow motorists.

Harry drove back to Loretta's.

He did not stop this time but cruised by.

A CLOSED sign now hung inside the front door.

Well, that made sense. To close down at breakfast, one of the busiest times of the day. Sure. Perfectly normal.

He kept on cruising, turned at the corner, drove to the alley that backed the block, turned there, and drove to Loretta's rear entrance.

He picked up his car mike. "Inspector seventy-one reporting a possible two-eleven in progress at three-oh-six Broadway. Will investigate. Over."

Harry got out of the car, took a step, then stopped. He turned, reached back into the car, and extracted the coffee container. Then he walked to and through Loretta's back door into the kitchen area.

It was empty. No cook. No cutters.

Then he heard voices. Male. Harsh. Jumpy.

"You did good to tell he was heat."

"Yeah, lady. You handled the cop real fine. Now keep doin' fine and empty the register into this sack. Everybody else, stay smart and stay alive. This bag'll come your way in a minute, so get yourselves ready. Don't waste no time. I want your wallets, rings, watches, necklaces, everything. Into the bag. Now. Quick. *Move* it."

"And you, mama, you come with me. We're gonna party."

Three voices.

Harry drew his gun from the shoulder holster in his left armpit. It was a devastating weapon. A black long-barreled model 29. A .44 Magnum.

He dropped his hand to his side, angled the gun out of sight behind his leg, and casually stepped into the coffee shop.

Everyone froze.

Dozens of eyes turned his way and widened. Harry was interested in only three sets.

He made one man at the space between the front door and

the front window. The lookout. Smart guys. Keep that front door covered. And the back? Shit, we're goin' out that way. The lookout balanced a sawed-off double-barreled shotgun on his thigh.

Harry spotted the bag man, the leader, in the right corner of the shop, taking up his collection. He clutched what Harry figured to be a .38 in his right hand, but he also held that sack with both hands. Brilliant tactician.

The third punk—the joy boy—was closest to Harry.

He also clutched a handgun, but his hands and mind were much more occupied with the pretty young woman he was dragging to the kitchen area.

Three big-timers. Real pros. Yeah.

Harry leisurely moved around to the front of the lunch counter.

The leader finally broke his trance and spoke. "What the fuck you doin', chump?"

Articulate. As well as clever, Harry thought.

He lifted the coffee container.

"I've been coming here for almost ten years now and every day Loretta there"—he nodded pleasantly at Loretta, who didn't twitch, blink, or breathe—"gives me a large black coffee. Today she gives me a large black coffee with sugar. Lots of sugar. I thought I'd bring it back and complain to the chef."

The joy boy yelled, "What the fuck you talkin'?"

"Well, fellas it's like this." Harry calmly set the too-sweet coffee on the counter. "We're not gonna let you just walk out of here."

"We? Who the fuck's we, sucker?"

Even the lookout was interested now.

Harry paused, marking the distances.

"Smith . . . Wesson . . ."

Harry swung the Magnum up into sight.

". . . and me."

The three gunmen reacted immediately.

As did the almost-victims.

The lookout hefted his shotgun, swiveled away from the door, and let loose with both barrels at Harry.

The customers and shop employees panicked. Their control, their patience, their nerve, collectively broke. Earlier, when the robbers had first made clear their intent, each person in the shop had recognized that she or he was in the presence of death. But it was still remote. It was closer, but they refused to believe that it was anything more than a possibility. And it's always a possibility. But now it was different. Now death was at hand. Violent, unexpected, messy. Death. It was standing in their midst. The realization was more than they could bear. So, as a group, they cracked. Some, women and men, screamed. Most leaped from their seats and ran. With little plan and no direction. Others dived to the floor. A few sat straighter and screamed louder. All panicked.

There was chaos and pandemonium and, most of all, fear.

The shotgun blast exploded the lunch counter beside Harry and to his right into thousands of shattered pieces.

Harry held his fire. He had to be careful. The anarchy of the scrambling, terrified people cut low his return-fire potential. He knew the lookout would reload immediately. That meant some leeway. A couple of seconds at least. So Harry ignored him and leaned in front of the blasted section of counter.

As he did, the area directly behind him, a pie case and mirror, blew apart as several cross-fired slugs ripped into it.

Slivers of glass and chips of plates sprayed out in every direction.

Harry could hear the joy boy's special victim scream even louder. He knew she'd make a break. Now was the time. Probably her only chance. And that would leave her attacker vulnerable.

She broke and Harry pumped a quick shot at the punk. He scored but not with a kill shot.

He then spun, crouched low, and fired at the leader. The bullet caught the would-be robber chest high, whirled him around, and whacked him over a table.

Another double-barreled blast splintered the counter on Harry's other side. This one was close, he noted. Too damned close.

Harry popped a shot at the lookout and splattered his throat. The punch of the bullet slammed the shotgun man back against the wall, where he slid, quite slowly, to the floor and gurgled away his life in great red gobs.

The screaming of the innocents escalated and transformed itself to wailing.

The joy boy was on the floor, gun still in hand, wrestling with the now-hysterical young woman.

Harry was anticipating a clear shot when he heard the sound of pistol fire and felt a surge of hot air blow by his head.

He spun to see the staggering, bleeding leader aiming at him for another try.

Harry fired twice. In quick succession.

The first bullet lifted the leader up off his feet and the second sent him crashing through the luncheonette's front window.

Suddenly, in the wake of the two Magnum explosions and the crystalline smashing of glass, there was silence.

Panic had moved beyond the stage of vocal expression.

The air was filled with the acrid odors of cordite and fear.

Harry turned back to the last punk. The joy boy was stumbling to his feet, desperately fighting to control the young woman. He needed a hostage badly. It was his only hope.

The punk had both arms wrapped tightly around the battling woman with his gun hand at the level of her hip, the barrel of the gun angled downward.

Harry extended his arm, pointing the Magnum straight at the struggling couple, who were locked in a spinning, grunting embrace.

The joy boy began to drag the woman toward the front door.

Harry yelled, *"No."*

The punk stopped, gaped at Harry and at the Magnum. The woman, with a supreme effort and a last, desperate hope, controlled herself and stopped fighting. Then she let herself go limp and sagged against her assailant.

Joy boy was suddenly off-balance; his shield had become a dangerous liability in an unexpected way. She was dragging him downward, exposing him to the brutal handgun. He was off-balance, caught in mid-action, like a rabbit at night on the highway, frozen in the headlight beam of an oncoming car. His gun pointed neither at the woman nor at Harry. It aimed at nothing.

He clutched the woman tightly and leaned backward, doing his best to drape her body over his.

Bearing her full weight, he stood very still. Sweating. Bleeding. Thinking.

The only sounds in the shop were the tinkle of tiny bits of

shattered glass falling to the floor and the punk's labored breathing.

Harry stood, unblinking and perfectly still.

From a distance, he could hear the treble whine of sirens. They grew louder, shriller, closer. Tires screeched; car doors opened and slammed. Footsteps bustled.

Harry knew there'd be cops all over the place now.

And he knew the punk would know it, too.

Would he get smart or suicidal?

Harry cocked the Magnum.

Joy boy body-twitched and squeezed his weapon.

In a low, calm voice Harry told him, "Go ahead. Make my day."

Joy boy dropped his gun.

Cops engulfed him and led away the young woman. She had begun to cry, softly.

Harry lowered his Magnum and exhaled a long, slow breath. He looked to his side. His jacket was torn ragged.

He walked back to the blasted counter and retrieved his coffee. It had survived the carnage intact. He called over a passing uniformed patrolman.

"Bag this and sent it to D'Ambrosia. Ask him if coffee's psychic."

The night was clear and brisk. The sky was a deep, dark blue-black, cloudless and speckled with flickering stars. A vigorous breeze blew in from the bay. There was even a quarter-moon crescent.

It was definitely one of those San Francisco nights that brochures and travel books brag about. The air nearly crackled with a seemingly electric energy. There was excitement tonight in the city. It promised adventure, romance, experience. It was a night that one could believe in. A dreamer's night. A night when anything could happen.

But all this was lost on the two men sitting in a nondescript black Chevrolet on posh Nob Hill, across from the Mark Hopkins Hotel. They were just tired and bored and doing a job. One man, Ernie Jacobs, all sharp angles of knees and arms and nose, slumped in the driver's seat, wedged under the steering wheel. His companion, Cletus Barnes, a black man, younger and rounder, focused his gaze on the hotel. It was his duty to watch the entrance, but at the moment he was attempting to meditate his way through a diet crisis. It wasn't working very well. Jacobs belched.

"Ernie?"

No reply.

"Ernie? You sleepin'?"

Jacobs turned on his side and cocked an evil eye at Barnes. "How the hell can I, you keep peckin' my ass every fifteen seconds?"

"You hungry?"

"Hungry? After that grease-drop soup you mooched from your brother-in-law's chinketeria? I'll be tastin' that sludge for days if it don't give me the runs."

Barnes smiled. "Then I'll grab you some rolls of TP on my next coffee go."

"Very funny. I should've known." Jacobs belched again. "A six-foot-six, three-hundred-pound *schwartze* chef in a Chinese restaurant."

"It was free."

"You got ripped off." Jacobs settled himself back for a nap. "He should've paid you."

"Ernie, if you're gonna sleep, at least open your window. You won't have control. I'll need me some cross ventilation. I don't want to get farted to death on duty. Won't look right on the commendation.''

Jacobs belched and then growled, ''Go to hell.''

Barnes laughed heartily and returned to his task. He and Jacobs were part of an ongoing special-unit investigation of organized crime. Years before, it had been a genuine and sometimes productive endeavor. But with recent cutbacks and realignments, it was now just a token effort. He and Jacobs mostly did surveillance. On a lot of different people, a lot of different places. It was dull duty but it was safe. Tonight they were watching the comings and goings of a particularly vicious and eminently successful crime boss.

Barnes suddenly sat up in his seat and squinted at the hotel's entrance.

A plain brown Plymouth pulled up to the hotel and a tall, lean, very fit man exited the car and spoke a few words to the valet parker, who approached him.

Barnes slapped Jacobs on the side of the thigh. Jacobs immediately began to protest profanely, but Barnes cut him off.

''Ernie.'' His tone was serious. ''Lookit. At the entrance. Is that who I think it is?''

Jacobs craned his neck to look. ''Oh, shit.''

The man walked into the hotel.

Harry crossed the ornate, elegantly furnished lobby and headed for the main ballroom.

He'd had it with the bullshit, the red tape, the bureaucracy, the frustration. It was time to make something happen.

As he hit the threshold of the lavish ballroom he heard music. A waltz. Played very well by a rather large orchestra for a wedding reception. Well, nothing's too good for the best, he mumbled to himself.

A Japanese woman materialized suddenly at his side.

"May I see your invitation please, sir?"

Harry looked into the room. The waltz was still playing. Gowned and tuxedoed guests were assembled in a large circle. In the center of that circle a white-haired, very tanned man of slight build and height danced with a young, dark woman. The man danced slowly but with much grace and expertise. The woman wore white lace. She was a bride.

"May I see your invitation please, sir?" The Japanese woman was young, polite, and good-looking. Damned good-looking.

Harry reached into the inside breast pocket of his sport coat and tugged out his ID. He flipped it open and held it in front of the hostess' face.

"I don't . . . understand," she said, looking at his shield and reading his card. "Inspector . . . Callahan."

Two tall, husky men in dark three-piece suits appeared on the ballroom side of the doorway. Their hands were clasped in front of them in the classic fig-leaf pose, and each wore a large fresh pink carnation.

Harry eyed their thick necks and bullet heads. Without looking at her, he addressed the hostess. "Do you know San Francisco General's emergency number?"

"Why, yes . . . I do," she replied.

Harry slid his badge into his side pocket. "Call them. Tell them to send an ambulance here. Tell them to expect two sorry-looking assholes with multiple contusions, various abrasions, and a shitload of broken bones.

The huskies squirmed and moved forward.

"Inspector Callahan."

The huskies halted and looked over to a dark, curly-haired

man of middle age and aquiline features. He wore a stylish black tuxedo, a wing collar, a bright red box tie and cummerbund, Gucci loafers, and a small red rose boutonniere.

"Mr. Loomis, we were—" He silenced the husky with a patrician wave of his hand. "How may we be of assistance to you, Inspector?"

"I'm here to see Threlkiss."

Loomis's eyes widened. "At his granddaughter's wedding? On what business?"

"I want to help him catch the garter."

"Inspector, even you should know that there are harassment laws." His tone was less civil now.

"Excuse me." Harry stepped through the trio and crossed the ballroom. The huskies started to pursue but Loomis stopped them. He followed Harry himself.

Outside, in their unmarked, Jacobs and Barnes wondered what to do. Jacobs was philosophical.

"*Shit*. Why me? On a nothing detail. A lousy, goddamned peeper tour."

"What do we do, Ernie?"

"We call Briggs. Let him decide."

The music had stopped. Threlkiss had proceeded to his table to rejoin his wife, grandchildren, nieces, nephews, cousins, grandnieces, grandnephews, and assorted huskies of various shapes and sizes.

Loomis caught up with Harry just before he reached the great man's table. "He's not a well man, Callahan. Another time, another place. He's had too much excitement today as it is."

Harry ignored him and stepped directly in front of Threlkiss and faced him across the table.

Loomis kept the goon squad calm with a slight shake of his head.

Threlkiss, with some assistance, seated himself and looked up at Harry.

"Well, well. Harry Callahan. Sit down, please." He reached for a fluted wineglass. A lackey instantly poured champagne. "Champagne, Harry? It's imported."

Harry stared at him. Threlkiss sipped.

"Men, Harry, like wine, should grow finer with age, more civilized. They should mellow. Become more . . . worldly."

Harry continued to stare. Threlkiss coughed.

"But, alas, not you, Harry. Never you. You are the one constant in an ever-changing universe."

He drew a dark brown cigar from his jacket and offered it to Harry.

Harry ignored it. Threlkiss smiled as he shook his head. A lighted match appeared. Threlkiss puffed the cigar to life. The flame and match vanished.

"So, Harry—"

"Linda Doker."

Threlkiss stopped puffing. His smile faded. He stared at Harry now.

"That name supposed to mean something to me?"

"She got fished out of the bay last month with her breasts slashed, her feet burned, and her face smashed to pulp."

Threlkiss resumed smoking. "Oh, yes. I read about it. Hooker, wasn't she?"

"Yeah. With a hefty price tag. Her specialty was making old scumbags mellow and worldly."

Threlkiss blanched under his tan, coughed cigar smoke, and spilled ash on the pleated front of his starched, diamond-studded shirt. He waved the cigar in the air. Hands took it from him and brushed away the ash.

Harry smiled. "I think she had a special customer who told her things."

"You're a fool, Callahan."

"I think maybe she got clever and wrote those things down."

Threlkiss's face tightened.

Harry reached into his coat pocket and pulled out a fat, crinkled white envelope. He held it up in front of him. For all to see.

"Maybe she made a copy. Maybe she didn't tell about it when she was getting coat hangers jammed up between her legs."

Threlkiss flushed red; his eyes bulged.

"What do you think the scumbag's bosses will do when they find out? Maybe he's got a family. Maybe his ass is in the ringer."

Threlkiss began to tremble. He started to rise from his chair. Hands tried to assist him but he pushed them away.

"You fucking bastard." His tremble got much worse very quickly. His breathing became shallow and rapid.

"You fucking *bastard*." He staggered backward as he screamed at Harry. Suddenly he clutched his chest.

Harry turned and walked away.

A rush of people surged in the opposite direction. A woman screamed. The bride ran across the room.

Harry kept walking.

In the lobby Harry spotted two men, one white, one black, running in from the street. As they saw him they opened and lifted their identification. The white guy spoke to him. "Sorry about this, Inspector, but Captain Briggs says to—"

"Ernie." The black guy had discovered the tumult in the ballroom and was already running toward it. The white guy excused himself and ran after his partner.

"Inspector, what's going on?" The Japanese hostess had materialized again. She was very concerned.

"Somebody grabbed his chest."

"What? Do you mean someone had a heart attack? What happened?"

"I think he got the bill for this party."

Harry handed her the worn envelope and walked away. The hostess was bewildered and hesitantly opened it. When she saw the pages inside, she was even more confused. She looked around the lobby for Harry but he was gone. Her brow wrinkled as she took the pages out of the envelope and unfolded them.

They were blank.

3

Less than ten hours later, Harry pulled into the parking lot of the Cliff House. Though the morning was bright, crisp, and sunny, Harry could not share its zest and promise. He hadn't slept. He needed a shave and a change of clothes. He'd spent the night filling out reports in triplicate and swilling the homicide squad's ammonia-flavored coffee. He sometimes wondered what the hell that pisswater was doing to his stomach if it corroded the coffeepots so badly that they needed to be replaced every few months. But, so what? Whatever gets you through the night. Maybe he'd head over to Loretta's if Briggs didn't haul his ass over to headquarters. Harry knew a blowout was on the way, but he hoped Briggs would wait to do it the second thing that morning.

Harry then remembered his last visit to Loretta's. No, Loretta's was out for a while. Closed for remodeling. He'd have to find another spot for the interim.

He left his car and waded through the crowd of reporters,

photographers, scene men, coroner's people, orderlies, drivers, and spectators.

Pretty damn big crowd for eight A.M.

Harry walked to the center of everyone's attention. A black Caddy that had seen better days.

A short, burly, rumpled detective intercepted him. Ed Sebastian.

"Hey, Harry, wait till you see what we got here. Stiff got himself a thirty-eight caliber vasectomy."

Harry grunted as he noticed that Sebastian was chomping on a "foot long" hot dog smothered in ketchup. Shaking his head, Harry continued on to the car.

As he did, a slender, young blonde woman dressed in jeans, a maroon ski jacket, and running shoes detached herself from the crowd. Her features were slightly angular. Her blue eyes large. Her skin was smooth and very white. She walked briskly away from the crime scene.

Sebastian caught up with Harry at the car. "Hey, Harry, you don't look so hot. What, big night? All noogied out?"

Harry peered inside the car. A fat, rigid body was hunched down under the dashboard. Its lower half, particularly at the crotch, was crusted with dark blood. Its face was frozen in shock, pain, and death. A toupé had slid halfway down a large forehead that was startingly punctuated by a round red hole.

Harry laid his hands on the car roof and sighed. He stretched his neck, first to the right, then to the left. He did the same with his hips.

"So what do you think, Harry?" Sebastian was still gnawing on his hot dog. "Gang hit, screwed-up drug score, unlucky john, Zodiac's back, or an unhappy faggot love affair?"

Harry turned his head to glare at the squat detective. He

noted the hot dog and walked away. Sebastian trailed him to the cliff edge.

"Don't tell me this shit's gettin' to you. Not Harry Callahan. Not Dirty Harry. Say it ain't so."

Harry stared out at the sea.

"No, it's not getting to me—the shootings, the knifings, the rapes, the old ladies getting their brains mashed for their Social Security checks. Teachers getting tossed out of fourth-floor windows because they don't give everybody an *A*. Babies getting toasted in microwaves because their mother's afraid she's gonna lose custody. That doesn't bother me a bit."

Harry's voice was getting tenser, louder.

"Hey, Harry, c'mon, take it easy."

"Or this job, either. Every day having to wade ass-deep through the pus and scum of this city. That's nothing, rolls right off my back. And the best part of all, the losing—getting swept away by bigger and bigger waves of corruption and apathy and red tape? No, that doesn't bother me a damn. But you know what does get to me? What makes me sick to my stomach?"

Sebastian's jaw was slack. He'd never heard Harry talk like this. Hell, no one had. And now he was about to share a confidence. Shit. Wait till the boys at homicide hear about this. "No, Harry, what?"

"Watching you stuff your face every morning with hot dogs and ketchup. Nobody eats hot dogs with ketchup."

"What the hell you talkin' about?"

"I'm talking about sticking our fingers in the hole while the goddamned dike's falling apart."

Harry fell silent.

Sebastian did, too. He started to bite down on his hot dog but reconsidered and tossed it down into the water.

After a moment the quiet was ended by the approach of a uniformed patrol cop.

"Inspector Callahan? Captain Briggs says to get your ... self over to the commissioner's office right now. On the double."

Harry nodded. The commissioner's office.

"Swell."

The blonde woman steered her metal-gray Oldsmobile Firenza through the growing rush-hour traffic on Gough Street and turned left on Union. She began to search for a vacant parking space and counted herself lucky to find one almost immediately. She left the car, fed the appropriate change into the meter, and walked to the next block.

This section of Union Street had been rather recently metamorphosed. The former barns, carriage houses, and gingerbreaded Victorian dwellings of Cow Hollow were now part of a walker's paradise, a strip of stylish specialty shops, intriguing bookstores, intimate restaurants, and handsome gift shops. There was also an art gallery. Masterson's. It was the woman's destination.

Although it was still early, the imposing green-and-cranberry converted Victorian was bustling with activity. A troupe of college-aged artsy-craftsy men and women were sweeping and dusting, arranging and hanging, doing all the things that needed to be done in order to open a new exhibit.

The blonde woman stopped before the large front bay window and observed two men balancing a large painting on a tall, sturdy easel.

The painting was spectacular. It was a vibrant swirl and dash of exploding color and motion. Although it was abstract and seemingly formless, its intensely passionate textures and brushwork gave the impression of forming, then fading objects and images. Eyes, hearts, skulls. Faces seemed to change expression. It seemed to move, transform itself, soar, then return to its original inert state. Its colors—black, purples, grays, reds—pulsated. They seemed to stretch against the force of the painting itself as they strained to hold back the power trapped in the physical materials of paint and canvas.

It was a uniquely eloquent expression of profound pain and despair.

The young woman's reaction to all this was a very slight smile shaded with pride and satisfaction. As her gaze shifted to the lower-left corner of the work, to the small, almost imperceptible JS, her smile grew a little larger.

She left the window and entered the gallery. She stopped beside a large A-framed placard just inside the doorway. It proclaimed, in large gothic lettering, that a DARK VISIONS exhibit was to open that evening.

The blonde woman scanned the hustle and sighted a short, plump, older woman supervising the work. As the older woman went to a desk to consult a sheath of papers the young woman approached her.

"Leah, can I speak with you, please?"

The older woman looked up, surprised but happily so. "Jenny. What marvelous timing. Look, we're setting 'Remembrance' in the window. I'll take it out tonight, of course, and give it the favored position on the west wall."

The blonde woman smiled as she shuffled her feet. "That's kind of you, but I'm afraid you'll be wasting a good selling spot."

Leah came around the desk and forthrightly grasped the younger woman's shoulder with a chubby hand. "Nonsense, child. It's the jewel of the exhibit. Don't be discouraged if it doesn't sell immediately. It's so intense. People will take time to get used to it. To tell you the God's honest truth, I'm just getting used to it myself. You don't know how many times I asked myself how such a howl of anguish can come from such a sweet girl as you.''

The younger woman bowed her head, uneasy with the compliment, but offered no answer to the question.

"I'm leaving town,. Leah.''

"No—when?''

"Today. Now.''

"But you *can't*. You'll miss the opening.''

"I'm much better at the painting than the reception. Can I leave you an address where you can send the paintings when the exhibit closes?''

"Of course you can.'' Leah cupped the blonde woman's face in her hands. "But think positive, my dear. It's money we'll be sending you. From the sales.''

Leah patted the other woman's white cheeks and turned to fish out an index card and pen from the clutter atop the desk. She handed then over as she asked, "Where will you go?''

The younger woman wrote for a moment, then handed the card and pen back to Leah.

"Up north. To visit someone.''

Jenny was in her car, stopped at a red light. She was thinking. She had much to do.

She was also remembering. Someone. Someone very special.

Four young self-styled studs came into her line of vision as they crossed the street. They ogled and whistled and hooted at every attractive woman who walked by them.

Jenny watched.

The studs noticed her watching and surrounded her car.

The apparent leader was all taut skin and shiny hair and thick, wet lips. And tight, bulging pants.

He leaned on the driver's door, leering in at Jenny, and stuck out his thumb in the hitchhike sign.

She looked up at him.

He ran a fat tongue around his protruding lips.

Jenny smiled up at him. Innocently. Invitingly. She rolled down her window.

"Need a lift?"

The leader swaggered and shot a look at his grinning cohorts.

"Sure, baby," he slurred, bending down so that his face was level with Jenny's.

The light turned green.

Jenny inclined her face out the window, close to his.

"Then stick a jack up your ass."

She gunned the car out from under his grasp and away. As he stumbled, dodging the now-flowing traffic, his friends mocked him.

Harry was seated in a kid-soft leather armchair in front of a huge oak desk. The burnished dark wood was flawless. Its luster so deep and brilliant that Harry could see he looked like hell. He still needed a shave and a meal and a sleep. But he wouldn't be getting any of them for quite a while yet.

Briggs was just building up a good head of steam.

Across the desk from Harry sat the police commissioner, a well-groomed professional man in his mid-fifties. A police commissioner had to be many things to many people. Sometimes these "things" conflicted with one another, sometimes they crashed into one another, yet somehow this particular commissioner kept them from canceling one another out. He was political, yet frank and fairly open. He was tough but not yet cynical. He believed in image maintenance and public relations, but he also believed in cops.

"Are you aware that you destroyed months of surveillance and intelligence work? Thousands of dollars? Hundreds of man-hours?" Briggs went back to pacing. "Special Investigations has been busting its ass preparing a case against Threlkiss."

The heat in Harry's belly was getting hotter and it was spreading. "Which he would have snaked out of. Maybe I did you a favor. I know I saved the taxpayers a bundle."

Briggs stopped short and exploded. "By Jesus, I've good reason to bust your ass down to traffic or, better still, kick it off the force. You're a dinosaur, Callahan. Your ideas don't fit today."

"And what ideas would they be, sir? That murder is against the law? That it should be punished?"

"Don't lecture me, you son of a bitch. Do you know who you're talking to? Do you know my record?"

Harry turned away from him.

"Yeah, you're a real legend in your own mind."

Briggs took quick jumping steps in Harry's direction. Harry kept his seat but reflexively tensed.

"God damn you, Callahan."

The commissioner spoke up. "Gentlemen. That's enough."

Briggs fought to control himself, walked to the wall of windows at one side of the office, and scowled at the city. Harry relaxed.

After a moment the commissioner went on. "Inspector, your methods are unconventional, to say the least. You get results, but often your successes are more costly to the city and this department, in terms of publicity and physical destruction, than most other men's failures."

Lieutenant Donnelly shifted his position on the couch. "Commissioner, Inspector Callahan—"

"Please, Lieutenant. The press will have a field day with this latest episode. And it comes so closely after that coffee-

4

Jenny gave a last, longing look at the ocean, trying to draw on its strength and serenity. She loved its infinite blueness, its endless stretch and width. She loved the hypnotic wash of its waves. If only she could siphon its relentless purpose and deep, unshakable determination. She'd need much of both qualities in the days ahead.

She turned off the beach highway and drove up into the woods. Most people found this silent, shaded area a restful and tranquil retreat. But not Jenny. She hated its darkness and shadows. She dreaded its quiet and stillness. She'd come here so many times before, but it was never any easier.

She followed a curving road over and around some hills and came to a small grouping of low granite buildings. Their arrangement and construction was unobtrusive and almost pleasant, but there was, nonetheless, no doubt about their institutional function.

Jenny parked in the visitors' area and sat for a moment,

clutching the steering wheel and holding her breath. It was always the same. Fear, sorrow. An almost insurmountable urge not to go in. To turn away. To flee.

But she always fought the anxiety, conquered the fear. She always went in.

She exhaled, released the steering wheel, and climbed out of the car.

Jenny walked down a long antiseptic corridor. There had been a concerted effort to brighten it up, to camouflage cheerfully its true nature, but the bright colors and childlike drawings didn't quite succeed.

Jenny passed several open doorways. She did not look into them. She knew only too well what she'd find. The specifics, the faces, the identities, might change, but the reality was always, tragically, the same.

There were patients in those rooms. Here they were euphemistically referred to as "clients." In the various stages of their maladies. There were often nurses or attendants to care for them or simply to keep them company. There was desperation in those rooms. Loneliness. Sometimes she tried to console herself and pretend that there was no conscious suffering, that drugs nullified the pain. These clients were not physically afflicted. But who, outside of the experience itself, could know the true essence of profound mental disorder?

She always tried not to think of this but she always did.

She was escorted by a short, wiry, white-haired, white-bearded man. He was explaining to her, in a subdued tone.

"Your sister's condition remains unchanged. Physically she is as well as can be expected, but she continues in a static, vegetative state. Elizabeth is totally unresponsive to the external world about her. But please, Jenny, understand, we are, as always, hopeful."

They had arrived at the end of the corridor. They were

standing in front of a closed door. In the door there was a small window.

"I'll leave you now. But please come see me before you go. All right? Promise?"

Jenny nodded. "Yes. Thank you, Dr. Barton."

When the man had ambled away, Jenny moved up to the door and looked in.

She saw a spotless white room. A perfectly made bed in the center of it. Off to one side a large window through which poured a shaft of golden sunlight. And in front of that window, sitting in that sunlight, in a high-backed, long-armed Naugahyde chair, a very pale, frail Elizabeth.

She wore a white lace-collared robe and fuzzy white mules on her feet. On her lap lay a fluffy gray stuffed toy. A koala bear.

Jenny entered the room.

She crossed directly to her sister and knelt before her. She leaned close to Elizabeth's face and looked long and deeply into her eyes.

Their faces, white and smooth and soft-featured, were variations on a single theme.

After a time she spoke.

"Hello, Beth. It's me, Jenny. How are you, honey?"

There was no response. Jenny expected none.

"You look so pretty. I've missed you."

She lightly caressed her sister's cheek. Elizabeth stared straight ahead.

Jenny rose and circled behind her sister. Standing in the same radiant wash of sunshine, she gazed through the window at the same distant horizon Elizabeth contemplated.

"Beth, I saw one of them. He appeared. In front of me. I thought I was having some horrid, evil vision. But no. He was there. Older. Uglier. I followed him. For days I watched him.''

Jenny paused.

"And I bought a gun.''

She bent over the chair. Her face hovered over Elizabeth's.

"I followed him to a bar. I let him pick me up. I let him drive me to a dark spot. We were alone. I let him think . . .''

Jenny closed her eyes.

"It was like I was outside myself, Beth. Above me, looking down. He played music. The same song. Then he touched me. And I killed him.''

Jenny moved in front of her sister. She knelt again and took Elizabeth's hands into her own.

"I know what I'm going to do now, Beth. For the first time in a long while, I know.''

Jenny leaned over to her sister and gently kissed her cheek.

"I'm going now, Beth. I love you.''

Jenny rose and nearly ran from the room.

Elizabeth continued to sit in the sunlight. She did not move or utter a sound but shed a single tear.

Harry was ending his first full day of forced inactivity. He hated it. Vacation. Bullshit. No way. But he knew he had no choice and he hated that even more. But there were limits. They could force him to take his two days off from last week and stack them against this week's. But that was it. Four lousy days.

He left the Ferry Plaza Restaurant and walked out toward the first level of the Golden Gate Ferry Terminal. He hadn't done much of anything all day except catch up on some badly needed sleep. At dinnertime he had driven over to the restaurant but, once inside, had changed his mind. He was in no mood for crowds of people having a good time. Maybe he'd stop at Procopio's Market on the way home and pick up some of their prosciutto and mozzarella. And a couple of loaves of that crispy Italian bread. That would do nicely with a few cold beers.

As he thought about it he decided that it might not be such a bad idea to stock up a bit on groceries. He rarely food-shopped because he ate out so often. Mostly on duty, while running something or somebody to ground. Maybe it was wise to stick close to home for the rest of his off-time. If he could keep from going stir crazy. That way he could avoid the regulars who knew him and who hung out at the same bars and restaurants he frequented. Word must be out already—it moved so damned fast—that Harry Callahan had gotten his ass chilled. He'd be swamped by the curious. This way he'd skip all the bullshit questions about the bullshit situation he found himself in. Then, when the days were up, he'd go back to work. The commissioner and Briggs and Donnelly be damned. It was his job. It was how he defined himself. So he'd get on with it. If the wide asses and pencil pushers didn't want him to do it, they could damn well fire him and be done with it.

The evening air was cool and damp, and just beginning to gust in off the bay. Harry was thinking about Procopio's marinated mushrooms as he walked to the Transit District's parking area when he felt a familiar little prickling sensation at the base of his neck.

What the hell was this? Time off? Vacation? Bullshit.

He looked around but saw nothing unusual. The ever-present sightseers and nightwalkers were moving about, but that was common. Couples, in all possible combinations, were standing by the water, gazing at the sky, the bay, the wharves, Oakland, and each other. But not necessarily in that order of preference. Traffic was moving slowly. Condition normal.

He figured he was just rammy from his big, fat nothing day and crossed the street that curved around the terminal. As he neared the center dividing stripe he heard the sudden, angry bass rumble of a high-performance engine that was being pushed to its limit. He spun around and saw a black limousine launch itself in his direction.

He could do nothing but leave his feet and jump-roll out of the barreling car's collision course. His left leg burned. He'd just made it. The car's front bumper had clipped his thigh.

From the ground, flat on his back, Harry twisted around to look at the car. It screeched to a halt, screamed a reverse, and spun around for a second go. It was on him almost as quickly as his perception of its intent. He rolled away from the killer wheels. On his stomach, he saw the flash of shiny hubcaps zip by his head. They continued a few feet and then spun again, skidding, the tires savagely biting the ground for traction.

Harry jackknifed up to one knee and reached for his Magnum. Before he could unholster his weapon, the car zoomed straight at him. It was so responsive and the driver so good that the radius of action was phenomenally small. All he could to was fling himself out of its lethal path.

He rolled away from the phantom killing machine and kept on rolling, across the remaining section of street and directly under a late-model Coupe de Ville that was illegally parked outside the ferry terminal.

The limo shrieked, whirled, and slammed into the Caddy.

Harry drew his Magnum, rolled out from under the opposite side of the car, and came up firing. He popped three rounds, point-blank, at the car's windshield.

Nothing happened.

He heard the bullet impotently ping as they ricocheted off the dark-tinted glass.

Then the car's front passenger door flew open and a burly guy in a dark blue warm-up jacket jumped out. Shielding himself behind the door, he fired a rapid-shot burst at Harry with an Uzi machine pistol.

A straight line of jagged bullet holes ripped across the Coupe de Ville.

Automatic weapons, Harry noted. Swell.

He ducked, swung around the end of the car, and fired at the Uzi man. His bullet bounced harmlessly off the limousine's door.

The driver's door opened and the driver let loose at him with another murderously rattling Uzi that tore another deadly stripe in the de Ville.

The back doors opened and a third and fourth assassin, armed with pump-action shotguns, blasted two loads at Harry that blew out two huge chunks of the now-demolished parked car.

Harry swung out again and emptied the Magnum at the killers, who hunched down behind their doors. No result.

He dropped to one knee to speed-load, an art at which he was expert, and heard doors slam and an engine rev.

He took off, running into the terminal, across its first level, and up its stairwell to the second deck.

The narrow walkway stretched out in front of him. Except for a few covered aluminum trash cans to one side and a large wooden dumpster a little farther along on the other side, the concrete thruway was completely empty.

He heard the squeal of the limo's tires and the roar of the engine. He leaned over a steel railing and looked down to see the car skid to a stop at the side of the terminal and three of the assassins jump out and run for the stairwell.

Harry turned and looked at the long empty space in front of him.

The assassins raced up the stairs to the second level and peered along the walkway. No Harry. Carefully they began to move forward.

The center killer nudged his partners and nodded at the dumpster. The three men smiled and advanced to the large wooden container. On a signal from the center man, they barraged the dumpster and pulverized it.

Only when their Uzi and shotguns were empty did they cease firing.

The center man stepped up to the mangled container and slowly lifted its lid with the end of his shotgun barrel.

Harry popped up out of one of the aluminum trash cans behind them and instantly dropped the man at the dumpster.

The other men spun around quickly. Before the second shotgun man could aim at him, Harry fired and blew him into the splintery remains of the shredded dumpster.

The third killer was trying frantically to reload his Uzi but never made it as Harry's third shot opened his chest, which instantly spouted blood.

The limousine started up.

Harry jumped out of the trash can and dashed down the stairway to the ground level of the terminal. He was too late. The assassin wearing the dark warm-up jacket sped away toward downtown. Harry watched his red taillights escape and disappear among the countless other lights of the city.

Lucky man. He got out with his life. This time.

Harry knew he'd have another chance at the crud because he knew there would be another try. After all, the guy probably had nothing else to do. There was no more Threlkiss. And no more cigars to light.

Harry holstered the Magnum and thought about Procopio's. He hoped they were still open.

The next morning, Harry found himself sitting in front of Lieutenant Donnelly's desk. He was doing a lot of this sort of thing lately. Too damned much.

Donnelly was a slender man of medium height. His sandy hair had been thinning out for the last few years. Soon it would be a memory. A twenty-year vet (he'd started later in life than Briggs), he'd done enough things right (or wrong, depending on your point of view) to rise to the rank of lieutenant, but he (and everyone else in the department) knew he would go no further. He was a good enough man. And a good cop. At least, he still tried.

He was staring into an untouched cup of coffee. He had offered Harry none. Harry knew that was supposed to mean he was ticked off.

"Hell of a way to spend a night off, Harry."

"You joining the act, too?"

"No, I'm not, for Christ's sake. Back off a little. I'm worried about your ass. You're going to get it shot off or kicked out of here."

"What else is new?"

"Harry, be serious, god damnit. These bastards are not hyped-up junkie half-wits. To their minds, you killed Threlkiss. Same as if you pulled the trigger. They are not going to stop. They're going to keep coming after you."

"Good. That way we'll know where they are."

Donnelly shook his head. "You're incredible, Callahan." He started to rearrange some papers on his desk. "You're also on vacation. As of right now."

"I'm not up for vacation."

"You *are*, damnit. I just put you up. Now go grab yourself

some R-and-R. And, for sweet Jesus' sake, stay out of trouble.''

Harry stared at him.

This was outrageous and unacceptable.

But they had him.

Or did they? He'd give it some thought. Some serious thought.

He rose, went to the door. As he opened it Donnelly called to him, ''You hear me, Harry? Peace and quiet.''

Harry slammed the door as he left.

5

Harry needed to get out of town. Not for the safety. Not for the peace and quiet. Not for any of the bullshit excuses the idiot brass threw up to keep him from doing his job.

He needed to get out of town because he had some work to do. And some thinking.

So he drove out on Route 101 north, up toward Santa Rosa, then turned east and headed toward Jack London State Historical Park. A few miles before the park entrance, he curved around a hill and entered a small wooded area at the base of a moderately steep hill.

He stopped the car, went to the trunk to unload his gear, and walked into the woods.

It was early and the morning was bright. But the trees were tall and thick with branches and leaves. This made for a dark, heavy shade. But Harry had no difficulty. He knew the spot well. He'd worked and thought here many times before. He found the path easily.

In a few minutes he came to a small sunny clearing. He put down the gear and started to set up.

He picked up a long white rolled length of paper, a hammer, and a box of tacks, and walked across the clearing. He came to a large wide tree, unrolled the paper, and tacked it to the tree.

He went back and repeated the action twice more, with two more rolls and two different trees.

Returning to his gear, he lifted a handled canvas duffel bag and turned back to survey his work.

Three black man-sized silhouettes faced him. Targets.

He bent to unzip the duffel. From it he slid a polished, rectangular mahogany case. He opened it.

Inside was a gleaming .44 Magnum automatic.

The only one of its kind.

Harry had received it as a gift. The grateful husband of a hostage and potential murder victim was a master gunsmith. A few months after Harry had rescued his wife from the mess of a botched bank robbery, he had sent him the boxed gun and a card that read, "You saved my wife's life. Maybe this will help to save yours."

In his time as a cop, Harry had never accepted a thing, not even a free cup of coffee. But he accepted this gift.

It was a fearsome weapon. It was quicker and more devastating than his model 29. It fired more shots, nine. And it took a special powder grind and larger load. It was, indeed, the most powerful handgun ever made.

Harry lifted it out of the box, hefted it, and sighted along its long barrel. Then he reached for its clip.

And heard car sounds.

Back at the dirt road, beyond the wooded area, a red Datsun 280ZX coasted to a stop. From it stepped a tall, broad, thick-muscled black man. He looked around, then leaned into the car and reached into the back seat. He withdrew a huge black pump-action shotgun. Its barrel was long and wide. He reached into the pocket of his dark brown windbreaker and pulled out four shells. He loaded the giant weapon, pumped a shell into the chamber, and thought about adding an extension to the barrel. He decided against it and rested the gun in the crook of his arm, then quietly stepped into the woods.

He advanced slowly, peering through the shadows, listening for sounds, searching for a path.

After walking several yards, he heard a sound, a twig snapping, to his left. He stopped, scanned the area, and listened hard. Nothing.

After a few feet he heard another sound, a branch and leaves rustling, this time off to his right. He stopped. Looked. Again nothing.

Then he heard a sound behind him. He whirled. Nothing. Then another sound, behind him again. He whirled around, got his legs and feet twisted under him, stumbled, and sat down hard on the damp ground.

A shadow passed over him and he looked up.

Right into the barrel of the Magnum automatic.

Harry stared down at him.

"Morning, Horace."

The black man's shocked face widened into a smile. "Sweet Sister Sadie's slit. Where the hell'd you get that?"

Harry lowered the gun and helped Horace to his feet. "I've had it. Figured it was time to get used to it."

"Damn, Harry." Horace brushed off the seat of his pants. "I saw the car. Fuckin' fabulous when the slime come after you in tanks."

"More and more are being made. For kings, sheikhs,

big-business hotshots, and hoods. They're almost impregnable to anything less than artillery."

Horace laughed aloud and pointed to the automatic. "Well, shit, you got that covered now."

Harry smiled and nodded at the shotgun. "Let's go see what they can do."

Back at the clearing, Horace demonstrated the power and accuracy of his weapon. It was devastating. He blew out the entire midsection of a target and ripped open the tree behind it.

"Not bad," Harry complimented him.

"Not bad, your ass, jamf," Horace hollered. "You'd have to strain the remains for fingerprints."

Harry slid a clip into the automatic.

"I heard you're taking a little vacation." Horace watched Harry heft the gun, gauging its balance. "I know a real nice place you can stay."

"You heard wrong."

"You got no choice."

"Maybe I do."

Horace frowned. "You don't mean quittin'?"

"I'm thinking about it."

Harry raised the gun and fired four quick shots. He peppered the heart area of a man-shaped target.

Horace smiled. "Damn, you got the feel."

"Not quite."

Harry emptied the clip at another target. He polka-dotted the silhouette's head.

"You know, you quit, Harry, and the department's up shit's creek. Who the hell's the brass gonna blame for their ulcers?"

Harry reclipped and fired again, alternating shots at the right and left targets.

"And what about the PR guys, Harry? They're gonna miss

strokin' all them feathers you ruffle and, shit, they'll have to leave off kissin' them big hairy asses you're always kickin'."

Harry reloaded, set the gun down in its open case, and hoisted the last remaining piece of unused gear. A large, heavy, metal plate. He carried it toward the center target.

"And what about all the interns at the emergency wards?" Horace said, following him. "There goes all their practice on busted heads. And the bandage factories—you jamf, don't you know there's a recession on?"

Harry placed the metal plate against the middle tree, directly in front of the man silhouette, then returned to his fire point.

Horace followed him back. "Cut the jive, Harry. You're a cop. It's all you'll ever be and it's all you'll ever want to be."

Harry looked at Horace. His friend wasn't joking now. His face was quite serious.

"Thank you, Doctor," Harry said as he picked up the Magnum.

"Shit, Callahan, they cut you, you bleed PD blue, jamf."

"Don't count on it. And what the hell's this 'jamf' stuff?"

"It means you're a jive-ass mother—"

"Never mind."

Harry positioned himself. He eyed the plated target and the two others. He lowered his weapon to his side, set himself, and snapped to action, firing until his gun was empty.

Then he lowered his arm and peered at the targets to assess his accuracy.

The unplated targets were perfect hits, head and heart.

Horace whistled loudly and ran to the plate. The bullets had pierced the metal. He shoved it aside and checked the silhouette.

The hits were dead on.

He whooped, jumped in the air, and threw a clenched fist in the air.

Harry looked down at the automatic in his hand.

"Almost there," he said softly.

There were other routes that Jenny might have taken: 101 part of the way, 17 all the way. They were probably faster. But she had no desire for speed. She had waited a long time. And without even knowing she was waiting. Time had become a drug to her, she realized. A heavy narcotic that blurred the past. That blunted the searing hurt with layers of distance and cooled it to a dull ache. Time, lots of it, thirteen years, had helped her contain the horror and the pain. Helped her hide it away. But now she knew it had not dissolved or expired. It was still there, deep within her. And it had grown. It had become hard, durable. And patient. Very patient.

So Jenny drove along Route 1. She thought and planned and remembered. But the memory was only of Elizabeth. In the years after. The years ahead. And now. They were all the same. Silent. Motionless. Unconnected. Jenny wondered what thoughts, what feelings, if any, her sister might have. Did she remember? Did she hurt? Did she feel anything anymore?

Jenny shook her head to clear her mind of these thoughts. She had no need of them now. She was committed to a course of action. She'd follow it through to wherever it led. She must put aside sorrows and doubts, and get her job done. It was time. After all the years. Now. It was time.

She turned and gazed at the ocean. The sun was setting. The sky was fading from high blue to orange to red to purple. This was the reason she had chosen Route 1. To be as close to this as she could. The sky and the sea. At that moment the sun slid into the boundless ocean. She watched it and drew on it for strength and resolve. She breathed deeply.

Jenny turned back to the road. A sign up ahead marked her destination. San Paulo.

San Paulo.

She drove away from the ocean and into the small seaside town.

San Paulo. Thirteen years.

She followed the highway through the patchwork conglomeration of dwellings. Some clapboard and run down. Others wooden and superbly kept up. Some large and stone. Others small and glass and very avant-garde.

She turned right on Bay Street and angled out past the hospital and onto Beach Street. She drove by the oddly combined motels and hotels. Some brightly painted, sprawling stucco terraces with a three-star French or seafood restaurant at ground level. And others gray, boxy, down at the heels, and without even a coffee shop or snack bar.

She slowed as she came to a line of structures across the street from the motels and hotels and at the head of the beach.

She could see the ocean. She could hear the surf.

Standing before her were an arcade, a ballroom, and a multiride amusement area, crowned by a huge, winding rising-and-dropping roller coaster.

Jenny stopped at the point where the buildings began. She knew that on the other side there were gift shops and corn-dog stands, T-shirt stores and cotton-candy counters, soda fountains and hit-the-bottles, break-the-balloons, ring-the-posts games.

She also knew that beyond them, just before the sand and the beach and the water, was a boardwalk.

And, under that boardwalk, a dark, deserted area. Covered with kelp and driftwood, and spiked with broken shells.

Jenny stared at the breakers.

She could feel the pinch of the shells, the grind of damp,

coarse sand. Little hurts compared to the others. She could smell the fishy, salty odor of decay. Pleasant smells compared to the others. She could see the damp, brown, splintery boards above her. Beautiful sights compared to—

Jenny heard a grunt. Far off. Thirteen years away. She heard more grunts. Animallike sounds. Then a groan. A disgusting satiated noise. Then more groans, more grunts, sniggers, and giggles.

A song was playing on a radio.

The Beatles. "Long and Winding Road."

A scream began.

It was suddenly cut off by a—

Jenny shivered. She shook her head. She was sweating. All the creases of her body were moist. Her face was clammy. Her hands were clamped, white-knuckled, to the steering wheel.

She gasped a chestful of air and held it. Then she exhaled, relaxing her hands, and sank back into her seat.

She looked out at the sea. It was still there. As it had been then.

She drove away.

Jenny and the woman carried in the last of Jenny's few belongings. The house was small. Smaller, actually, than some apartments she'd rented. There were a tiny kitchen and bath, a small bedroom, and a good-sized living room/parlor. But the house was right at the cliff edge. There was nothing below but rocks and waves. At low tide there'd be some scant square feet of beach, but that was unimportant to her. What mattered to Jenny was that the house stood alone on this, the shoreward side of the road. There were a few other houses like it but they were up the road, around a bend, and out of sight.

And, of course, she loved the wall-to-wall floor-to-ceiling window at the seaward side of the house. It gave her a perfect view of the ocean from living room and bedroom. And the natural light was spectacular. Just the right thing for her painting. Although her new job would monopolize most of her day, she had ideas for new personal projects.

Her stay in San Paulo would serve her. This time. In many ways.

The woman set down a suitcase. "Miss Spenser, I really can't tell you how glad the historical society is to have you. Your letter came at exactly the right time. I swear it was serendipity. We count ourselves fortunate that you were available. Your work is so impressive, so impeccably authentic."

"Thank you. I do my research."

The woman clasped her hands in front of her and leaned forward on her toes. "Well, now, I hope the house is suitable. It's a wee bit deserted out here in West Cliff, but you said you appreciated solitude. And I can understand that. After all, you'll be seeking inspiration and—"

"The house is lovely."

The woman opened her arms. "The fridge and cupboard are stocked. There's wood for a fire." She dug into her bag. "And, since you know the way, here's the key to the carousel house." She handed it over. "Everything you need should be there, but if you require anything further, we have an account at Dunstan's. I promise not to fuss, but please feel free to call me anytime. Let me know how you are progressing. And, of course, if I can help in any way, just yell. Well, then, that's it." She extended her hand. "Welcome to San Paulo and good luck with the project."

Jenny shook the hand. "Thank you."

The woman sighed dramatically. "It must give you a great

feeling of satisfaction, making old, ugly things right and pretty again.''

Jenny looked her in the eyes.

''Yes, sometimes it does.''

The woman let go of her hand and left the house. As her car put-putted away in the distance Jenny walked to a puffy old parlor chair that was turned toward the window wall.

She carried a small twine-tied box.

She sat in the chair, placing the box on her lap. She untied the twine and lifted the top away. Inside, an object was wrapped in white cloth. She removed the cloth to expose a .38 Colt.

She stared at it. She looked at its shiny, silvery metal.

She heard a song playing.

She saw bodies. In a dark space.

They were pressing against each other. Pushing.

She heard grunts, snickers, groans.

She heard tearing.

She felt damp, cold air. Harsh, gritty sand. Mucky sea-weed. Cutting shells.

She saw a belt unhooked. Eagerly, hurriedly.

A bra strap and cup is yanked down.

A small breast is exposed.

A girlish hand instantly covers it.

The hand is pulled away by rough male hands.

A skirt is ripped.

Panties are tugged down.

Girlhands try to pull them back up.

Malehands grope. Roughly. Probe. Uncaringly.

Faces. Boyfaces are vague. Indistinct. Yet brutally gleeful.

Jenny saw her own face. Younger. Frightened.

It is punched.

She felt the pain.

And saw another face. Even younger. Just as terrified. Elizabeth.

Jenny saw Elizabeth begin a scream.

The scream is cut off by the ugly, thick, clamping hands.

The scream.

It was more than a scream.

It was a word, a call, a plea, a cry, a prayer.

It was a name.

Jenny.

6

Harry was driving around, bored and angry.

He couldn't stand his apartment anymore. He never spent time there anyway. He worked. He did the job the taxpayers paid him to do. And he wasn't doing it now.

The only reason he put up with the endless hassles of the bullshit bureaucracy was that in the end he had his work to do. His job.

But now they'd screwed that, too.

Maybe it was time to pull the plug.

Yeah, he thought. And do what?

Harry turned right at the end of Columbus Avenue and hooked around Leavenworth to Jefferson. He followed that to the Embarcadero and decided to follow its curve.

He had already passed Fisherman's Wharf but he didn't much care. He wasn't in the mood for all those bright lights. He wanted the starkness and clarity of the old port part of the road. The deserted warehouses, the inactive piers, the stretch of waterfront that was unlike the picture postcards.

As he bounced along the neglected, potholed street, he did not see the old yellow Chevrolet convertible idling at the point where Bay Street ran into the Embarcadero.

He didn't see the car, so he couldn't have seen the three guys lounging in it, sipping from individual brown-bagged pints of cheap, raunchy bourbon. Hawkins and his pals.

But they saw him.

They rammed their overcharged vehicle into gear and shot after him.

Harry heard them first, then he glanced in the rearview and saw them coming.

He half smiled. All right, you simple-looking bastards. Maybe it was time to finish it. Maybe a little action would be just the tonic he needed.

The Chevy overtook his Plymouth quickly. A short, skinny freak was at the wheel. A tall, thick freak was beside him, and Hawkins was kneeling on the back seat.

Harry gunned ahead.

They roared up beside him, screaming, hooting, waving their arms. Then the driver sideswiped him hard. He bounced off their hit but regained control quickly. They bumped him again and dropped back directly behind him.

The driver accelerated and rammed the unmarked police car's rear. The car shot ahead with the additional external force, but Harry rode out the push and kept from swerving.

Both cars were flying now.

The Chevy butted him again. Harry felt the innards of the unmarked strain. He was jolted forward, his chest jammed against the steering wheel. His head whipped back as the car's engine raced to catch up with the speed at which its body was hurtling.

Harry searched in the rearview for the punks. They were not behind him. They were pulling up beside him again. The tall, thick one was in the backseat now, sitting, hugging Hawkins at the waist. Hawkins was leaning out of the car and swinging a long iron crowbar.

Hawkins pounded the back, the roof, the sides, and the front of the unmarked. He smashed out the side windows across from Harry. Shattered glass exploded into the air.

Harry wrapped an arm around his face to protect his eyes, then yanked his wheel to the right. The slam sent the punks squealing away, but the driver quickly recovered and shot out a half-car length ahead of Harry.

They were whooping and hollering and making faces. Hawkins was waving the iron. The driver then started to angle, just slightly, toward the water.

They were going to run him off. Slowly. An inch at a time.

Harry floored his gas pedal and smashed them head-on. They bounced away, swerved around once in a complete circle, and gunned back at him.

Who the hell was training these goddamned drivers? First the one in the assault car and now this son of a bitch.

They pulled up beside him again. Hawkins slammed the crowbar into the windshield.

With a deafening crunch, the window spiderwebbed into thousands of pieces.

Harry drew out his Magnum and knocked out a section of the fractured glass so that he could see.

He was about to fire at the Chevrolet when a flickering light came at him. It flew right through the smashed-out side window. It rolled on the floor under the dashboard, beside him. He looked over. It was a Molotov made from a strip of shirt and a pint of cheap bourbon. It was flaming.

Harry snatched it and flung it out his window.

It blew up and shot off a sheet of fiery light.

Harry could hear other thudding, glass-breaking sounds. They were pelting him with their empties.

Harry looked up ahead and saw the wide gray support pilings of the Aerial Highway. He accelerated and swung between them, fighting the car's suicidal urge to fishtail.

The punks stayed on his ass as he approached the underside of the bay bridge. Harry figured they'd make a move.

They shot up beside him. Hawkins tossed another Molotov and they dropped off. The burning bottle of alcohol flew into Harry's back seat.

He arched back to grab it but couldn't reach it.

The punks rammed his side and tossed another flaming bottle, into the front seat.

The support columns of the bridge zoomed closer.

Harry fought the car with one hand and snatched at the Molotov in the rear with his other. It was no good. Each demanded his full concentration. He couldn't split his effort. One or the other would get him.

The concrete colonnade in front of him decided him. He braked and started to skid. The rear of the car wanted to flip out in front of him. He countered its pull and hooked, dodging the column. He heard a bottle explode just as the back seat burst into flame.

He screeched the car to a long sliding halt and reached down to grab the Molotov beside him on the floor. Jumping clear of the burning car, he faced the oncoming punks. When they saw him standing there, the driver gunned the Chevy directly at him. Hawkins stood up, lit another Molotov, and held it high.

Harry gauged their distance and his time. Fire reached the gas tank of the Plymouth and the car exploded in a thunderous upsurge of flame. He ignored it, waiting for the punks to come into range. When they did he waited even milliseconds longer so there would be no mistake.

Then he pitched the Molotov at the speeding car.

Hawkins's and his cronies' eyes bulged.

The bottle smashed against their windshield and spat out a sheet of liquid fire.

The driver lost control. Hawkins dropped his fire bottle to the floor of the car as it flew, skidding and screaming, at Harry.

Harry leaped out of its way.

The car curved wildly as the driver yanked too hard on the wheel, trying to avoid a stone column. The car shot along a vacant pier.

Harry hit the ground rolling and bounced onto his feet in time to see the punks and their Chevy launch themselves off the pier and out over the bay.

For a split second they hung in midair.

Then Hawkins's last bomb blew.

A booming, crackling, blazing fireball was instantly doused in the dark, still water.

Harry watched the huge crane hoist the charred, dripping car out of the bay. Three body bags already lined the pier.

Donnelly was angry.

"So that's your idea of rest and recreation. What the hell's wrong with you? Briggs is going berserk and the commissioner's climbing up my ass."

"Sorry to hear it."

"God damn it, Harry. Can't you do anything the easy way?"

"Am I back to work?"

"Yes, damn it, you *are*."

"Good. I'll get to it."

"Hold it. It's not what you think. You remember the cock-shot stiff out by the Cliff House?"

"Yeah."

"He's been in the city a few years. Mostly clean but definitely out in the shade. He looks strictly small time but who knows, maybe he just never got caught." Donnelly started to fidget.

"So?"

"He came from San Paulo. Born and raised. I want you to go down there and pick up whatever background you can on him."

Harry's face tightened. "What the hell is this?"

"It's a murder case, Harry."

"You're shipping me out. I'm attracting a crowd and you're afraid of the fallout."

"God damn it, Callahan. I'm doing you a *favor*," Donnelly was yelling. "You're a walking, frigging combat zone. People have a nasty habit of getting dead around you. I don't want any civilians taking the fall. You want to work? Fine, work. You got your assignment. Now get the hell out of here and do it."

Harry stared at him for a long, silent moment. Then he turned and walked away.

"And take all the time you need," Donnelly called after him. "No need to hurry back. Maybe the sea air down there will agree with you."

Harry kept walking and mumbled to himself, "Swell."

Jenny rose early the next morning. Sunlight poured through the glass wall of her bedroom and warmed away the chill that had crept in during the night. Half awakened by the intense brightness, she had thrown off her quilt and stretched out in the strong beam to sleep a little longer.

She awoke rested and eager.

After a long hot bath and a strong mug of Twinings Irish Breakfast tea, she left the house and went to her car. She wore her maroon ski jacket, green GI pants, and running shoes.

The night before, she had parked in the short driveway in front of the low, narrow garage adjacent to the house.

Before getting into the car, she decided to check out the mini-sized garage. She'd expected to struggle with the door but was pleasantly surprised when it slid up easily. She stepped in and looked around. Except for a well-used miscellany of garden and household tools, the garage was empty. It would suit the Olds fine. She turned to leave and saw a bicycle wheel sticking out of a shadowed corner. She wondered if there was a bike attached to it. She dug through the clutter in the corner and found a weathered, dusty, no-speed Schwinn. The paint was chipped and faded. And the frame had seen better, undented days but it wasn't rusted.

It would be marvelous to bike along the cliff to work. She remembered a trail there. Coming home would be hard work, the uphill part. But she could use the exercise.

She sealed her decision by brushing away the dust on the seat with her fingers. She looped the strap of her bag over her head and across her chest and lifted a leg over the top tube of the frame. Hopping backward onto the seat, she found a pedal with one foot and pushed off with the other.

She was on her way.

She biked out of West Cliff into the wind. It was brisk and cool and straightened her hair behind her, and it felt wonderful. By the time she reached Beach Street and the amusement area her skin was warm and flushed pink.

She felt energized and alive. Ready to begin.

She coasted by a grouping of kiddie rides and foot-braked in front of the carousel house.

It was a large circular building with a sectioned roof that peaked high at the center. Except for the frame it was constructed entirely of glass. The curving wall of the building was clear glass, whereas the roof was a stained-glass spectrum of colors.

Jenny leaned the bike carefully against the glass front door and peered in at the carousel.

She had to take a step back in amazement.

The carousel itself was not huge; she'd seen much larger ones in the Midwest. There was a moderate amount of figures and they were not narrowly spaced. Sometimes they were so numerous and densely packed that it was impossible to estimate, without tagging, just how many there were. The size and the number of figures did not surprise her, but the variety of animals and poses did. It was a Noah's Ark menagerie of creatures. There were a horse, a tiger, a lion, a black panther, a baby elephant, and a wolf. And they were only what Jenny could see from outside. She'd bet there were a buffalo and a camel and a rhino, too. And the benches were not just benches, either. There was a chariot. A tiny pony-drawn wagon and a Yukon pack sled pulled by a sinewy husky. Each creature was lunging or running or cantering. They were all different. Frozen forever in a singular action. Even their expressions were different. Eyes, noses, mouths, were arranged in subtle variations.

Jenny snatched the key from her bag and hurried into the carousel house. She wheeled her bike inside the door and remembered the kick stand. It was there and it worked. Leaving the bike, she circled the merry-go-round and the other creatures. Her guess had been correct. There were a camel and a buffalo and a rhino. She also saw paint cans, drop cloths, and brushes. The supplies were neatly stacked at the far side of the wooden platform on which the animals jumped and gamboled.

The carousel was a masterpiece.

She'd had no idea. She'd worked on three others and done quite well. She even had the beginnings of a reputation. But it was strictly earn-a-living and travel-someplace-different work. She had applied to the San Paulo Historical Society because she knew they wanted to restore the carousel for its coming centennial summer. But her objective was not the work. It was something quite different.

But this was nice. She could enjoy this job. It would be difficult. The figures were pretty banged up. But it would be well worth the effort. She could make this carousel crisp and bright and magnificent again.

Something caught her eye. She stepped onto the carousel platform and walked to a faded, shabby figure. A unicorn. It was more run down than the others. More popular, she guessed. She ran her hand along its rough flank. Dried flakes of paint crumbled away.

Jenny removed her jacket. Time to work.

7

Harry entered San Paulo. He'd gotten a late start and twilight was approaching.

Although it was less than two hours south of San Francisco, this was Harry's first time in the small town. He didn't know much about it. But, then again, he figured, there might not be all that much to know. Like many other coastal California towns, it was nestled between ocean and mountains, and looked out onto Monterey Bay. He remembered that the University of California had a pretty big campus here. There had been some nasty riots back in the sixties. That was the sum total of his knowledge of this community. Well, he did know that one George Wilburn, late of life, San Francisco, and an intact three-piece suit, had been born and raised here. And right now that was all he cared about. Get a little background on Wilburn and get back to the real work.

He had decided to postpone any career questions until he got back to his regular duty. If he could ride out this bullshit and if they let him alone, he'd go on. For as long as he could. Until maybe the next time. Until Briggs or some other tight-assed idiot pushed him too far.

He was on his way to the police station and had a fair idea of the layout of the city. While negotiating the required series of turns right or left in his newly issued unmarked car, he came to a red light at a busy intersection. What looked to be the main lot for the town's bus system was here. Buses came and went. Or waited for their drivers, who had taken a break for coffee or a visit to the john. There were plenty of people. Also coming and going but mostly waiting. Next to the bus area there was a crowded pizza parlor. Good pizza or force of habit? he wondered. It was close to suppertime and he was hungry. The thought of a slice of extra cheese and pepperoni was appealing.

While Harry was starting to salivate at the thought of the hot pizza, he heard two unmistakable and all-too-familiar sounds. Shots. He looked diagonally across the intersection and saw a bank. Then he heard the alarm. A car was parked across from the bank. It was empty but its motor was running.

Swell, Harry thought. Just swell.

Sure enough, a bearded, baseball-capped man ran from the bank, waving a big Army-issue .45 automatic, heading for the car.

At that moment a police car pulled up and an absurdly young-looking, bespectacled San Paulo police officer jumped out to block the path of the running "alleged" bank robber.

The young cop had his police special in his hand but didn't use it. He commanded the suspect to halt. The guy shot him.

Harry pounded his gas pedal and whirled his steering wheel. The robbery suspect, and now alleged assaulter with a deadly weapon, was pointing his old cannon at the cop on the ground. Intent to kill.

Harry sped between the cop and the robber. The surprised gunman broke his aim, fired at Harry, but missed. Harry kept going and cut the man off from his getaway vehicle.

Seeing this maneuver, the robber took off.

Harry unholstered his Magnum and left his car to give chase on foot.

The guy was fast but Harry stayed on his tail. He hounded him around buildings, across streets, and through stores. The guy dodged and weaved smartly, keeping startled people between him and his pursuer. Harry couldn't risk a shot.

Harry wondered where the hell the rest of the local cops were. He hoped the department wasn't lying in the street back at the bank.

The robber ran along a narrow street to the corner and spotted a meter maid on a three-wheeled motorcycle. She was arguing with a woman who was protesting a parking ticket. He pushed the woman sprawling onto the pavement, pistol-whipped the maid off the machine, then hopped on it and took off.

Harry, breathing heavily, hit the corner just as the scum pulled out. He looked around.

Across the street, a beige jitney with the words SAN PAULO RETIREMENT HOME stenciled in brown across its side stood idling with its doors wide open.

Harry didn't hesitate.

He jumped into the jitney, cranked it into gear, and sped after the three-wheeler. As he screeched through a tight turn he heard gasps and screams from inside the jitney. He glanced at the large round mirror over the entrance steps and saw a group of senior citizens sitting behind him.

Retirement home. Swell.

He called back to them, "It's okay. I'm a police officer in pursuit of a robbery suspect."

One of the old men leaned forward in his seat and yelled back, "Shag his ass, son."

Harry smiled. A gentleman after his own heart.

As he gained on the three-wheeler the robber twisted and shot at him. The bullet popped out a hole in the jitney's broad, square shatterproof windshield. An old woman screamed. Another swooned. The same old man hollered, "*Nail* that son of a bitch." The jitney swerved onto a fancy street of posh shops and restaurants. Harry realized that they were moving against traffic on a one-way street. The smaller, more maneuverable vehicle had a clear advantage. It was time to end the game. He sped up and roughly bumped the three-wheeler ahead, forcing one of its rear wheels up onto the curb. The would-be robber reflexively yanked the machine to the right and accelerated. He bounced off the curb and momentarily lost control of the cycle. He slashed across an intersection and rammed into one of the circular arrangements of flowers and plants that lined the street and gave it the look of a country promenade.

Each arrangement was bordered by a sturdy three-foot-high brick wall.

The robber sailed over the three-wheeler and the wall to crash down among the flower pots and bushes.

Harry braked to a stop, ran out of the jitney, and jumped the low wall, unholstering the Magnum. He flipped the dazed perpetrator onto his back and shoved the barrel into his face.

"I guess I ought to read you your rights."

Sirens blared.

Harry reached into his back pocket and pulled out his ID. He opened it and stuck his arm high in the air. The suspect groaned and spat petals and bulbs from his bleeding mouth.

San Paulo police converged on the site and, with guns drawn, surrounded Harry and his prisoner.

The old man staggered off the jitney and called to Harry, "Best goddamned day trip I've had since they dropped me in that goddamned home."

A young blonde woman in a maroon ski jacket observed the scene for a moment, then turned away to enter Dunstan's Art Supply Center.

The San Paulo police station was not far from the fancy street where Harry had taken the suspect down. He'd learned that the street was called a mall, Oceana Mall, and that the police chief was called Jannings, Lester Jannings.

It was dark by the time they'd finished with the suspect and reached the station, a modest beige one-story bungalow-type affair with a Spanish-tiled sloping roof. The work area inside was mostly one large room divided by a long counter and filled with a half-dozen desks and a dispatcher's setup. Dominating the room, at the center of the rear wall, was a partitioned office of semiglass walls. A man sat there, hunched over a desk.

Jannings.

Harry wondered where the holding cells were. And whether they had a lab. Maybe there were other buildings or a basement.

Jannings's door was partially open, so Harry didn't bother to knock.

The police chief looked up at him. Jannings was about fifty-five, a thickset, bearish man with a full head of brown hair. His eyes were heavy lidded and the corners of his mouth drooped to give him a look of fatigue. Or sadness.

He eyeballed Harry. "So you're the famous Harry Callahan," he said quietly.

Shit, Harry thought. Not another attitude.

Jannings sat back and folded his hands on his desk. "I'll make this short and sweet and I'll only say it once. This isn't the big city and we don't need any hot-shit hard ass to show us dumb yokels how to do things. You're here on some pussy detail, so stick your nose to it tight and keep it there. You read me, Callahan?"

Harry eyed Jannings a moment, then saluted him with an index finger. "Aye, aye . . . sir."

Before the police chief could respond, Harry walked out of the office. He could feel Jannings glare at him as he crossed the squad room and exited the station.

He was hungrier. He still hadn't had anything to eat, but he decided to register at his hotel, dump his stuff, and then hunt for a decent bite. He'd made a reservation, at Horace's suggestion, at a hotel called La Bahía. Horace had bragged that it was right on the beach.

He stepped out of his new unmarked and peered up at his temporary lodgings.

"Damn you, King," he muttered. The place was a dump. A few steps up from a flophouse or welfare hotel. *Damn* that Horace. La Bahía was gray. Everything about it was gray. It had Moorish or Turkish or whatever spires and might have been something years ago, but now was definitely on the critical list. And to make matters more frustrating, it was stuck between two pretty nice-looking places.

Well, he'd check out the room, and if it was a sty, he'd switch to one of the better places. Briggs and his expense sheets be damned; he was going to be here only one, maybe two nights at the most.

He carried his stuff into the hotel.

After signing in and getting his key from a gray dozing desk clerk, he climbed the stairs to his room, 213. The second floor was gray, too. The carpet was worn and thread-bare in spots. The lighting was dim and the walls were painted in the best shade of lowbrow drab. It looked as if the whole place were fading away, out of existence.

Goddamned helpful Horace.

He unlocked the door and heard a noise inside the room. He put down his suitcase and duffel bag, and reached inside his windbreaker.

He swung the door open slowly.

Inside, his room was not gray. It was black. Dark.

He crouched and stepped into the room.

He heard a kind of growl, then felt a surge of movement.

He huffed as something or someone slammed into his chest. He fell against what sounded like a lamp as it hit the floor and then hit the floor himself. Hard, banging his head. A great weight was on him. He felt rough skin, wiry hair.

He was set for an attack but none came. His opponent was apparently content to try to squash him to death. He tried to roll right, then left, but couldn't budge. He was pinned. He felt a hot rush of truly rank breath as he searched in the darkness for what he hoped had been a lamp.

He found it. It was a lamp. He switched it on and looked up into the broad, hairy face of his assailant.

Above him, staring at him with red eyes, breathing a stench at him, was the biggest, ugliest dog he'd ever seen. It seemed to be part Rottweiler, part bulldog, and part grizzly bear. It was starting to show him its teeth when Harry noticed the bright red ribbon around its neck. There was a card, too. Very carefully Harry turned the card over and read, ''Something warm to get you through those cold but starlit nights.''

Harry recognized the handwriting.

''Horace,'' he yelled aloud. ''You darky son of a bitch. You motherless black bastard. You—''

The huge dog growled once, climbed off Harry's chest, and marched into a dark corner of the room. Harry went back to cursing Inspector Horace King's soul but stopped suddenly when he heard water sounds.

He knew it wasn't the ocean.

He angled the lamp to throw light on a far corner of the room.

The dog held his leg high in the air and pissed a stream against a chair.

"Swell," Harry snarled.

Jenny was staring at her face in a mirror. She had set the mirror on an easel. Another easel stood next to it. A large white empty canvas rested there. Jenny carefully studied her image. She was dressed in a white nightgown and robe. She was barefoot. An old radio was tuned to the classical-music station, which was playing Mozart. Jenny lifted a hand to the canvas and began to sketch the first lines of a face. Her face.

8

The dog caught on pretty quickly. Harry was surprised. He looked to be the stubborn type. After a few knee butts that were just as painful to him—the dog was hefty but evidently all hard muscle—the dog let him jog without jumping on him or constantly cutting across his path.

The beach, except for a few other joggers and some scavengers wielding metal detectors, was empty at this early hour. The sky was ruffled with white clouds, and the wind off the ocean was bracing.

Harry jogged toward the protruding arm of land that curved around the north side of Monterey Bay. A bicyclist was gliding along in the opposite direction. A girl, Harry noted. Or should he say a young woman. He was always forgetting about the movement. She was slender and, to judge from her pace, in good shape. Her wavy blonde hair breezed out behind her. Good-looking.

The dog had noticed her, too, and stood mesmerized by her

approach. When she pedaled even with them, he started to bark wildly and ran off after her. He moved very quickly for his size. Before she knew it and could react or evade, he leaped at her, knocking her and the bicycle to the ground.

Harry sighed and jogged up to the bike path. He bent to take the sprawled cyclist's arm to help her up and scolded the dog.

"Damn it, Pissface—"

The cyclist yanked away her arm and jumped to her feet. "*What* did you call me?" Well, Harry thought, a challenge.

The dog started to bark again. Loudly.

"The dog." Harry had to yell to be heard over the barking. "I was talking to the dog."

The cyclist was brushing herself off, adjusting her shoulder bag. "That your dog?"

"Why? You want him?"

She gawked at him. Just for a second. "Listen, buster, if you can't control him, leash him. There are laws. It's for the animal's own good." She frowned at the giant cacophonous animal. "*Quiet*," she commanded.

The dog shut up and sat down.

Harry marveled. "I guess you're okay."

She retrieved her bike and swung herself onto it. "I'm fine but you'd better get it together."

She pushed off and wheeled away.

Harry watched her and smiled.

Harry reported to the station. He wanted to pull the file, check their computer, if they had one, for any possible cross-references to other cases, and get the hell out of San Paulo. A few hours, maybe the whole day, if he really got serious and interviewed relatives or known associates. In any event, he'd be back in the city by noon the next day.

The station was buzzing. There were about a dozen officers and four civilian clerks at work. A sergeant with bushy gray-flecked eyebrows and a bristly mustache manned the counter that divided the large room into two unequal parts.

Harry stepped right up and reached for his shield. "I'm Inspector Harry—"

The sergeant's head bobbed up. "Callahan," he said, loudly enough for everyone else in the room to hear. The other cops and clerks stopped what they were doing at that moment and looked up. The sergeant smiled broadly. "We've been expecting you. Chief Jannings briefed us." He turned to a group of three officers over by the file cabinets that flanked Jannings's partition and lined the rear wall, and shouted, "*Bennett.*"

Jannings was in his office, standing in front of his desk. Watching.

One of the three officers at the files left his task and hurried to the sergeant's side.

"Bennett, show Inspector Callahan to his desk."

"Ah . . ." With an index finger the officer slid his wire-framed round-lensed glasses back up to the bridge of his nose. "Right, Sergeant." He looked at Harry. There was a broad white surgical patch covering the left side of the man's forehead. "This way, Inspector."

Bennett held the waist-high swing door open and admitted Harry to the territory behind the counter. Cop land. The inner sanctum. Harry followed where the young cop led. The other officers and clerks stared as Harry passed. Jannings still watched.

They crossed the squad room, angling toward the far-right corner. There, between file cabinets and the side wall, was a minuscule space into which had been jammed an Army-green metal typewriter table and a straight-backed wooden chair. On the table was a single thin folder.

Harry viewed his "office" and turned back to glare at the spectators. They quickly resumed their work.

The young cop shuffled his feet uncomfortably. "This is . . . it, Inspector."

Harry eyed him. Bennett squirmed some more. "The coffee room's through that door." He pointed to the other side of the room. "And the john's downstairs."

Harry walked behind his "desk" and opened the file. Inside was a single sheet of paper.

"Sir . . . if that's all . . . I'll get back to work."

Harry stared at the embarrassed officer, who turned away, walked a few steps, then stopped and returned. He was beginning to blush.

"That was nice work yesterday, Inspector," he mumbled. "I was the one . . ." He touched the patch on his head. "You saved my life," he blurted. "Thanks."

Harry stared at him.

Bennett tried to recover. "Right. If you need anything . . ." He stopped talking and hurried back to his work.

Harry picked up the single sheet of paper, scanned it, folded and pocketed it. He recrossed the squad room, pausing to look back at Jannings, who still watched. In a low voice just audible to those around him, he mouthed a word clearly, so that Jannings would understand.

"Asshole."

The cops and clerks peeked at him and at one another.

Harry left the station.

Mrs. Sara Wilburn lived in a modest wooden house in what used to be a modest neighborhood. Now it was struggling. Most of the people on her block had fought back by painting and scrubbing harder than ever. Many of the small homes were spotless and sparkling. But here and there the money and the hope had run out. The paint had flecked away. The wood had begun to warp and split. The trash had begun to pile.

Harry checked the address on the rap sheet and parked in front of a house that was just crossing the line, just beginning to lose the struggle. He left his car and tried to open the wooden screen door of the home but found it latched tight.

He knocked and got no answer.

He knocked harder and longer.

Finally, a short, heavy-set woman opened the front door and appeared behind the weather-scarred screen door. The sky had grown overcast and the day was getting grayer and damper. The inside of the house was dark and the screen door was dusty, but Harry could see the grim set of the woman's lips and the sallow color of her skin well enough.

"Mrs. Sara Wilburn?"

"Who are you?"

He showed his badge. "Inspector Harry Callahan. San Francisco Police Department. I'd like to ask you a few questions about your son."

"I have no son," the woman answered flatly.

"Yes. That's why I'm here. I'm working on the investigation of his—"

"You don't understand." She raised her voice slightly as she corrected him. "I have no son. I have had no son for a long time."

"The record shows that George Wilburn was born to Sara Wilburn on—"

"A son was born to me but he was taken away many years ago."

What the hell is this? Harry thought.

"By whom?"

"By Satan and his evil minions." She spat the words out. "I had a boy." Her eyes widened as she stepped closer to the crusty screen. "I bled and pained to birth him. A beautiful baby. I rejoiced. I tried to raise him up a good, God-fearing child but the agents of Hell were too clever, too strong for him. They turned his weak head. They took possession of him. They conspired to achieve him eternal damnation."

She was shouting now. Harry rocked back on his heels at the force of the outpouring. The emotion was wrapped in a hard shell of bitterness, but he suspected the soft feeling inside had not yet turned to hate.

"I warned him. I begged him. But he wouldn't listen to me. He had ears only for the demons." She calmed herself a bit. "So I cast him out. I lost my son."

"Mrs. Wilburn—"

She slammed the door on his question and him. As Harry walked back to his car he looked over at the house next door. It was still holding the line, still undefeated. Maybe the woman watching him from behind her screen door was, too. He went over to her.

She came outside to meet him. She was approximately Mrs. Wilburn's age, taller and thinner. She pulled a frayed old letter sweater close around her to ward off the chill in the air. Her body had lost its womanly roundness. She was all straight lines now. Her hair had once been black.

She smiled at him, a resigned, ironic smile. "You been hearin' all about the evil minions?"

Harry nodded.

"She goes on like that a lot now. Cooped up in that house all alone. Husband died years ago. Sometimes she screams . . . She wasn't always this way. She had a smile once, a laugh that could light you up like a Christmas tree."

"What happened?"

The neighbor woman looked over at the Wilburn house. "That lousy kid of hers. Don't let her act fool you. Him dyin' like he did . . . It maybe pushed her over the edge."

"Tell me about the son."

"He was a bum. Him and his crummy friends. Everybody knew—"

"These friends still around?"

"I guess."

"Who are they?"

She looked at him and spoke slowly. "I don't know and I never want to know."

"How do I find them?"

"Try Ginley's Bar. That's where she says George used to hang out." She turned back to her neighbor's home and listened. No sounds came from the dying house. She reached back to close her own front door. "I better go see if she's okay."

She went to her friend's door.

Harry went to his car.

San Paulo was an oddly mixed town. The young and the old were very visible. Often at the same places. Along the beach street. At bus stops. At the inexpensive food markets and department stores. Students from the U of C were everywhere and they fell into the usual groupings. The jocks, the egg-heads, the preppies, the day-trippers, the whole-earthers. But there seemed to be an inordinate proportion of long straight hair, granny dresses, sandals, and all the other accouterments of flower days gone by.

Maybe there was a time warp close by, Harry thought, and hippies were slipping in from that great Haight-Ashbury in the sky. He hadn't much cared for the look or the philosophy then, and he hadn't changed since.

San Paulo also seemed home to more than its share of affluent people and more than its share of those sinking away economically. Of course there had to be a middle here. The shop owners and restaurateurs and hotel/motel people were obvious, but the others were much less evident. It was as if they were hidden away.

A lot of the stores and restaurants were like that, too. They were fancy and expensive or funky and artsy or lunch-counter and burger-stand stuff. There was no easy in-between.

Harry supposed that the town's bars and taverns were the same. He had just entered Ginley's Bar, so he knew what the downside looked like.

After the Wilburn interview he'd gotten some lunch and gone back to his room to read the San Francisco newspapers he'd picked up outside the Greyhound bus terminal. He did not want to lock horns with Jannings again, so he decided to sift the computer the next day before leaving for home. He slept the afternoon away, woke to watch the San Francisco news on a TV in the Bahía lobby, then fed Pissface a couple of cheeseburgers before taking him for a walk on the beach.

At nine o'clock he was ready to try Ginley's for Wilburn's friends.

The bar really wasn't much different from any other cheap lowbrow joint anywhere else. It stank of spilled drinks, unwashed armpits, and rotted dreams.

Harry ordered a beer from the thick, olive-skinned, cigar-chomping bartender and surveyed the long narrow room. The crowd was moderate but seemed to be growing. The bar was taken up mostly by silent, stooping shot-and-beer men. Watery-eyed, stubbly men, sucking the last breath of life out of the half-inch butts they lipped so tightly. Mostly solos, mostly silent. A foot-wide shelf hung on the wall opposite the bar. A few doubles and one triple had stationed themselves here. To sip and smoke and mutter.

The clientele was mostly male. Women formed half of one double and a third of the triple, but they sat stone-faced and wordless.

At the back of the room, beyond the bar, two squarish men in old flight jackets and one in a short, worn car coat were playing darts. And knocking back shots and beers at too quick a pace.

As their blood-alcohol level rose so did their competitiveness and rowdiness. Their skill, however, decreased rapidly.

One guy, the smallest of the bunch, was getting louder and louder. He was the best dart player of the three and was easily beating the others. He began swatting and thumping his pals as he won each round.

Harry moved to another seat, farther down the bar. He wanted a better view of the game and the players.

He ordered another beer and suddenly realized that the thumper was a woman. Her reddish hair was tucked up under a dark blue watch cap, but her cloth coat swayed open to reveal full breasts beneath a blue work shirt and round hips under faded jeans. Her skin was fair and freckled. Her face at one time, or perhaps even still in unguarded moments, might have been attractive. But now it was hard and resentful. Her nose was defiant and her lips mean.

Her companions, in turn, aimed and threw. The first guy missed the board entirely and speared the wall. The second guy's dart hit the bull's-eye, but flat, on its side. It fell to the floor.

The woman cackled as she shoved her bleary-eyed opponents. ''That's it, turkeys. The next round's on you.''

The wall stabber rooted in his pockets. He came up with nothing but lint.

The woman lost no time. The sneering half smile faded from her face. She pushed the man against the wall and moved in on him.

"C'mon, dickhead, fork over the bucks before I kick your nuts up into your nose."

Nice, Harry thought, genteel. He guessed her age to be thirty-five or so.

She was shaking the guy by his lapels as he told her, "Got none. I ain't got any bucks. We pissed it all away, Ray." He found his rhyme amusing and singsonged it over and over. "We pissed it all away, Ray. We pissed it all away, Ray."

The other guy giggled. The woman whirled to face him. "How about you, jizzmouth. Pull somethin' outta your pants besides that wet string of yours."

He dug into his jacket pocket. "Ain't got much, Ray. We been here all day. And Benny won't run us no tab no more."

She advanced on him, holding out her hand. "Gimme what you got, twatlips, before I give your face its first period."

He handed her the money and sheepishly joined his dart partner.

She counted the few dollars and change, snorted, and yelled to the front of the bar, *"Kruger."*

When no one answered, she marched past Harry to address a sullen, beefy man on his right.

"Want to go a couple chugalugs for scratch?"

The singsonger whined from the corner. "What about us, Ray?"

"Suck my ass with straws, drunks," she snarled at the whiner. "Get your own. What do you say, Kruger?"

The man at the bar downed the remains of his shot, then put his nearly full mug of beer to his mouth and unhurriedly emptied it in one long swallow. He set down his glass and, with a swipe of an arm, wiped the froth from his mouth onto a greasy plaid flannel shirt sleeve.

"I'm outta here. Fishin' early." He backed off his stool and waddled to the door.

Ray had one last go at him. "Shit, Kruger, you're good for nothin' anymore." He did not hear or ignored her and went through the door into the street.

Ray slammed most of her money on the bar and called to the bartender, "Belt and brew, Bennyboy."

Then she spotted Harry and smiled. She moved a little closer. "Hey there, cutie, wanna buy me a drink?"

Harry shook his head no.

Anger flared momentarily in her eyes and on her lips, but she quelled it instantly and tilted her head up at Harry. "I'm Ray Parkins," she said in a boozy imitation of a coy flirt. "You wanna ask me somethin'? Go ahead, honey, you might get lucky."

"No thanks," Harry replied. "Only with humans."

The anger erupted fully this time. She curled a fist and threw it at him. He caught it in midair. She curled her other hand and threw that at him. He slapped it away.

"Not very ladylike."

She kicked at his knees. He stepped back to avoid her thrusting foot and yanked on the fist he still clutched in his hand. When she spun around, he whacked her ass hard with the side of his foot.

Yowling and with arms outstretched before her, she hit the floor with a thud and slid into the wall.

The crowd left its sipping and smoking, and stopped murmuring. They were staring at him.

Harry faced them down.

The bartender came over to the end of the bar. "You looking for trouble, pal?"

"I'm looking for friends of George Wilburn."

The crowd edged forward. A short, tiny distance. More of a lean than a step. A tensing rather than a moving. But Harry recognized the importance of the action. They were allied now. United against an intruder, an outsider. The passive lid capping their frustrations could be blown very easily now.

Things could get real ugly real fast.

"You a cop?"

"What'd he do?"

"What's it your business?"

They were making demands.

"He got killed. Somebody blew his balls off."

The crowd stopped moving forward. The hostility held.

Ray, now seated on the floor with her legs spread and her knees up, began to cackle a raucous laugh.

The crowd became unsteady, unsure of its purpose. Its energy diffused. Pent-up resentments and angers crawled back into deep, secret places to wait for a next time.

The drinkers and smokers and mutterers went back to their pastimes.

Harry looked around at them. They'd forgotten all about his humiliation of one of their own. They'd also forgotten or never knew or just didn't care about George Wilburn and his busted pipe.

He shook his head slowly.

Ray was still sitting on the filthy floor, laughing.

Swell, he thought. Just swell.

He left the bar.

9

Jenny sat at a small table she had placed by the window wall of her house. She stared out at the distant line where ocean separated from sky. Two slightly different shades of dark blue. The sun would soon begin to rise and project its reds and yellows and oranges westward. In the light of its full power, the line would separate two slightly different shades of light blue. So much power changing so much so subtly. So stealthfully.

She sipped the last of her morning tea, carried the cup to the kitchen, and rinsed it. She was dressed in a gray crewneck sweater, her maroon ski jacket, black corduroy jeans, and running shoes. Her hair was tied back in a ponytail. She returned to the table. On it lay the shiny .38-caliber revolver and, standing upright, six shiny cartridges. She picked up the gun and methodically inserted the bullets into the chambers of the cylinder.

Twenty minutes later, she was sitting in her Oldsmobile,

parked at the beginning of Beach Street, across from the San Paulo Pier. Her shoulder bag was on the seat beside her. It was still dark but Jenny could look across the bay and see grayness clinging to the outlying land at either end. That meant fog, regardless of which direction he took. Good. Fog would help.

She watched the entrance to the pier.

After a while she heard the grind of old gears and the cough of an old engine. She slouched down in her seat so that her head would offer no shadow or silhouette.

A beat-up green Dodge pickup bounced along the pier, turned right onto Beach Street, and chugged away.

South. She'd guessed wrong. No matter. She waited a few seconds, started the car but did not turn on the headlights, pulled away from the curb, glided through a U turn, and followed the truck southward.

The pickup stayed on Beach till it ended, then climbed up to East Cliff Drive and paralleled the coastline until it was out of the city and onto Sea Cliff Road.

Jenny followed at a comfortable distance. To her left, through the trees of the dense, tall woods that lined the road, she could see the dark blue of the sky growing lighter.

After about ten miles the road began to pull away from the shoreline. For the first time there were woods on both sides of the road. Narrow dirt trails now led off the road and down the steep decline to the ocean. Jenny saw the two red taillights of the pickup turn right onto one of the dirt paths and angle downward. Slowing down, she followed.

When she was close enough to see that the pickup had parked, she stopped. She watched a beefy, sullen-faced man exit the truck and begin to unload packs and cases.

She waited.

After three trips the man did not return to the pickup. She waited a few more minutes to be sure, then left the car.

She very quietly walked to the pickup, then followed the man's direction down to the sea. Soon she cleared the woods and looked out on a small rocky cove.

The hillside sloped to a small plateau just above the rocks and crashing waves. It was here that the man had set himself up. The sun was rising and quickly burning away the fog.

From the cover of the edge of the woods, Jenny looked down on the man. Kruger.

He was reclining on a short, striped canvas beach chair. To one side he had placed a large duffel bag and a rectangular cooler. On this sat an opened beer can. On his other side he had set a small-screen wireless television set and a series of tackle boxes, plastic buckets, and bait cans. At the plateau's edge he had placed three long fishing rods. They were standing upright, their grips inserted securely into three holes dug in the firm-packed clay. Their lines disappeared into the swelling, sinking surf.

Kruger reached into the duffel bag, extracted a Sony Walkman, and fitted the headset onto his ears. He spun dials for a few seconds, then laid the radio on the ground beside him. Next he reached into a pocket of his flannel shirt for a match and a joint. He lit up, inhaled deeply, and lifted his chin skyward as he held on to his hit. Finally he exhaled. Settling back into his beach chair, he pulled a magazine from the duffel, opened it, and sucked some more on the joint.

Jenny let him enjoy himself a little longer. She wanted to be sure he was set. When he was, she moved out of the woods, drawing her weapon from the bag that hung over her shoulder.

As she approached from behind she heard him making sounds. Odd, high-pitched sounds. Like whines or whimpers.

Then she noticed that his right elbow was moving rhythmically up and down. She assumed that he was vocalizing badly to the music only he could hear and that he was tapping out a beat with his right hand. But as she stepped closer she saw that she was mistaken. His right arm was working pretty good. She moved in behind him and saw that the magazine was opened to the centerfold, where a two-page spread presented the closest possible gynecological scrutiny of a woman's most private parts.

Jenny swallowed a bitter upsurge of acidic bile. She had to control her anger and her revulsion. She had to control herself to do what she must do. What she had waited all these years to do.

She extended her arm and pressed the barrel of the revolver against the distracted man's neck. He bucked in the chair, ripped off the earphones, and twisted in his seat.

The barrel of the gun now squashed his nose flat. Tinny, high-pitched country music leaked out of the headset.

His eyes bulged round and wide. His jaw became slack. His mouth fell open. Jenny fingered the trigger. Control the impulse, she commanded herself. Wait. Wait for the moment. Make him know.

"Turn it off," she ordered him.

He fumbled for the radio, switched it silent.

Jenny circled slowly to his front, keeping the round dark hole of the barrel pointed at his head.

He slid the magazine down to cover his crotch. "For Christ's sake, lady." He attempted indignation but failed miserably. He was too shocked and embarrassed. Too scared.

Jenny stared at him.

He looked from her face to the gun to her face. He began to sweat even though the morning was quite cold.

"You don't remember, do you?" she asked.

"Remember what? Please, lady—"

"My sister and I will never forget."

Jenny focused her eyes on his fat, frightened face, which started to melt into a younger version of itself. Her perspective of it altered. It was hanging over her now, flushed red and slick with moisture. Behind it was a black night sky dotted with twinkling stars. The face bobbed up and down as the body attached to it pumped back and forth. The eyes and lips were stretched wide in a malignant leer. Then, suddenly, they closed tightly, the body bucked once, shuddered, and went limp. The face grinned and let out a whooping noise.

Beyond the face and the noise, there was the sound of waves. Jenny heard them again. They washed away the memory.

"One night. A long time ago. Under the boardwalk."

Kruger's eyes changed. They didn't squint or blink or move. They changed inside.

"Remember?"

His fear was panic now, gushing, rampaging, hopeless panic.

He knew.

She lowered the gun and fired into the magazine.

Pages were torn apart. Blood spurted. He screamed.

She fired again. At his head.

He was quiet.

Harry and Pissface climbed the steps of La Bahía and headed toward their room. They'd had a good jog and Pissface had done his business. Harry had looked for the cyclist but she hadn't showed. He was damned anxious to run the computer check and get the hell out of San Paulo and back to work.

He had his key out and in the lock when Pissface went crazy. The dog started to sniff and growl and scratch the worn carpet in front of the door. Then he took off and scurried down the hall to another room and repeated his scratch-sniff-growl routine.

Harry reached inside his sweat jacket, unlocked his door, then bent and burst into the room. As he did there was a small *phutt* sound and the jamb of the door, at the spot where Harry's head had been, exploded into cracking splinters.

There was another *phutt* and then two quick booms.

The door down the hall flew open and a man in a dark blue warm-up jacket leaped into the hall with an Uzi machine pistol in his hand.

Pissface leaped at the man, jaws snapping, fangs flashing.

The assassin had turned the gun to blast the dog when Harry sprang back into the hallway, firing.

The man's chest popped open in two places as his body flipped up into the air and fell backward.

Harry looked back into his room, then at the body in the hall and the dog who was watching him, his eyes bright and his tongue hanging out of his mouth.

"Owe you one," he said as he holstered his Magnum.

A short time later, dressed in his sport coat and tie, Harry exited La Bahía. There was a small group of curious onlookers assembled on the sidewalk and an ambulance and San Paulo police car at the curb.

As Harry made for his Plymouth he looked across Beach Street, toward the amusement area. The pretty blonde cyclist was standing there, supporting her bike, looking back at him.

Their eyes met but they gave no sign of acknowledgment or recognition.

When she turned away and walked her bike toward the carousel house, Harry got into his car.

* * *

Jannings was not in his office.

Harry knew this as soon as he entered the squad room, but he figured he'd hang out a few minutes. If Jannings was in the building or close by, he'd get the word that Callahan was around quick enough and come running.

He turned away from the cops and clerks who were doing their best not to let him catch them staring at him, and scrutinized Jannings's office. There were the usual awards and commendations that adorn the office of any law-enforcement administrator. Also the requisite photos of Jannings shaking this guy's or that woman's hand. San Paulo big shots, Harry figured.

There were also a number of personal photographs. Actually, there were a lot. A little more than Harry usually saw in such offices. They were family pictures, mostly of a thin, shy-looking boy at various ages and sizes. Obviously Jannings's son. In many of the shots Jannings had his arm draped over the kid's shoulder. And Jannings was even smiling. There was the Little Leaguer/proud-dad shot. The young-camper/wise-pop shot. The spelling-bee-champ/father-of-the-victor shot, as well as others. In one the boy wore a cap and gown, and stood beside his beaming father. There was also a picture of the boy and five friends—four boys and one girl—leaning against a spiffed-up hot rod. They all hoisted beer cans in their hands and what Harry guessed were diplomas.

Harry crossed to the wall and studied the photograph. There was something about the girl and her haughty, challenging pose.

He was distracted by Bennett's breathless entry into the office. "Inspector Callahan, what—"

"Where's Jannings?"

"He's out at Buckman Cove. Some fishermen discovered a body out there."

"Jannings personally checks out every corpse that turns up?"

"Well . . . no, sir. But this was pretty clearly a murder."

"How so?"

Bennett nervously looked out at the eyes in the squad room. He lowered his voice. "Off the record, sir. The victim was shot twice. Once in the head and once in the genitals."

Harry's face tightened.

Bennett cleared his throat and spoke apologetically. "Maybe, sir, we'd better move into the outer office. Chief Jannings gets a little fussy about this sort of thing."

Harry watched him a moment, then pointed to the group photo. "Do you know any of these people?"

"No, sir. Not really. They were friends of the chief's son, I guess."

"What about the girl?"

Bennett raised his eyebrows. "Oh, you mean the bull— That's Ray Parkins, sir."

"You know her?"

"Well, everybody knows Ray. But she's nothing, just one of the town's . . . sluts. Why, sir?"

"No reason. She just looks familiar. I may have bumped into her or something."

Bennett nodded. "It's pretty hard not to if you spend much time in San Paulo."

Harry turned off Sea Cliff Road and drove down to Buckman Cove. There were policemen and cars, an ambulance, technicians, and, out on a flat piece of ground just above the rocks, Jannings.

Harry went straight at him.

"Why the hell didn't you call me?"

Jannings had been studying the corpse. His arms were

folded across his chest and his head was lowered. He looked up at Harry from beneath sagging eyebrows. He spoke slowly and quietly at first. "And just who the fuck are you that I should be calling you?" He was shouting now. "And what the fuck went on at your hotel this morning?"

Harry was a little surprised at the depth and meanness of the anger. He looked down at the body. Kruger.

"What's going on, Jannings?"

Jannings unfolded his arms. "You tell me, Mr. Big City Inspector. Everywhere you go something gets smashed or somebody gets killed. I don't like it. I don't like you. Finish your goddamned research and get the hell out of my town."

"It's not research anymore. You too stupid or just too pigheaded proud to see that?"

"Get out of here."

"The MO's the same. Ballistics will ID the bullet as coming from the same gun. I'll call—"

Jannings exploded. "You won't do one goddamned thing but get your ass out of here. *Now*. Right this goddamned minute. Or I swear to Jesus I'll lock you up."

Harry looked at the near-raving police chief. The man steadied himself, stopped his angry gushing, and stared back at him.

Harry left him and walked back to his car. Before pulling away, he looked down through the trees at the cove. Jannings was standing in front of Kruger's body. He was studying the dead man thoughtfully.

Ray Parkins hurried along Durfor Street to the hardware store at the corner. She entered and looked around. A sandy-haired, youthful-looking man stood near the plumbing section. Ray smirked when she saw the man and waited to catch his eye. He was slender and of medium height. He wore a knee-length powder-blue smock with the words TYRONE'S HARD-WARE stitched over his heart in a red curly script. He was with another man. A customer. When he saw Ray, he blinked as though startled. When she waved to him, he blinked again as though testing his vision. He excused himself from the customer and motioned to a young clerk to take his place. Then, with a nod, he directed Ray to the rear of the store. When they had circled behind a large shelving unit stacked with toilet seats of various styles and colors, he spoke to her in a harsh whisper.

"What do you want?"

"Long time no see, Tyrone, honey."

"I told you I don't want you in my store."

"I got to talk to you, you stuck-up asshole."

"We got nothing to say to each other."

"You hear the radio?"

"Leave my store."

"Kruger's dead. They found him this morning. He had his balls splattered all over the front of his pants."

Tyrone's pinkish skin blanched now. "I don't care."

"Same thing happened to Wilburn in San Francisco."

"Wilburn?"

"Yeah, remember him? He's dead."

"That's twice I don't care."

Ray stepped close to him. "You better care, prick. I think she's come back."

"Who?"

"Don't try to pretend, you hypocritical shit. You dipped your wick like the rest."

"Shut your mouth, you evil witch."

"What's the matter? Afraid somebody'll hear? Afraid you'll lose some of your customers if they find out?"

"There's nothing to find out."

"You make me want to puke. I'm gonna call Mick." She turned to walk away but Tyrone grabbed her arm.

"You do what you want. Just keep that psycho bastard away from me."

Ray yanked her arm out of his grasp and smiled. "I'll tell him you said that." Then she grabbed his crotch and squeezed playfully. "Watch 'em real good."

Tyrone shoved her away. She laughed her cackle. "And be prepared." She opened her jacket to reveal a gun stuck in the waistband of her jeans. Still laughing, she left him.

10

Van Burn was a small street running only a few blocks. It was a tiny needle in the huge, sprawling geography of the city of Los Angeles. It was a dusty, dry street that ran north from Hollywood Boulevard up into the Hollywood Hills. There it died, giving way to the winding hillside alleys that were called streets and the small stylish homes that were viewed from the sidewalks below as the trophies of success and happiness. Van Burn led up to that world but was in no sense part of it. It baked in the summer heat, choked in the smog, gushed a river in the winter rains, and was a tight, cramped conduit for the Santa Anas, the hot, dry, forceful winds that blew everyone in their path a little closer to his own particular edge.

The street was lined with small low-slung apartment houses. Triplexes and fourplexes. Even one eightplex. There were temporary havens for those hoping desperately to hang on. Illegal aliens crammed by the dozens into squalid rooms.

Whores, male and female, dozed, too punched out or too strung out to peddle. Companies of a chidren's army rested up for the coming night, when they could stroll the boulevard looking for that big break. People passed each other on Van Burn Street but didn't speak. There was nothing at all to say.

The jewel of the street, its largest structure, was the crumbling Shelbourne Hotel. Many hotels in Hollywood had backslid from a glamorous and prosperous past into a dilapidated, decaying present. But not the Shelbourne. It had always been a dump.

A skinny teenager with short slicked-back hair and wearing red high-heeled shoes clicked her way into the residential cheaper-by-the-week hotel and climbed to the third floor. She wore a black mini-dress that exposed most of her thin legs and clung to her flat, boyish behind. Before knocking on the door of room 303, she took the gum from her mouth and stuck it on the side of the doorjamb molding.

The door was opened by a scowling, shortish, muscular young man in his early thirties. He had broad shoulders that tapered to a tight waist. His head was large, his face broad. A pencil-thin black mustache topped a wide, thick-lipped mouth. Longish matted black hair fell over his high forehead and covered his ears. His eyes were large and dark brown, almost black. The white around the irises was tinged with red and shot through with ragged ribbons of blood.

Without a word he closed the door, walked across the shabby room, and sat down on a rumpled, unmade bed.

The teenager did not look around. She tossed her red vinyl handbag onto a chipped Formica-topped table and in a parody of sensuality turned her back, hooked her arms behind her, and slowly unzipped her mini-dress as she eyed the man from over her shoulder. Her face was powdered pale with uneven blush spots at her cheeks. Her lips were two red stripes.

She turned around and slid one shoulder of the dress off her own, then slid the other. The dress fell to her waist and, with a wiggle, she let it drop to the floor.

She wore a white low-cut bra that cupped her small breasts taut and high; tiny diaphanous panties; and white textured stockings held up by a lacy garter belt.

But her temptress' costume was flawed. The cloth of the bra was yellowed. The fabric of the panties had been torn away from the elastic waistband so that spots of white skin peeked through puckered holes. The garter belt was frayed and the stockings were seamed with runners.

If the man noticed, he did not acknowledge these defects. Nor did he comment on the fading circles of purple and green that the girl wore on her rib cage and upper thighs. He registered no emotion at all.

The girl stepped out of her mini-dress and clunked in her red shoes across the buckled, cracked linoleum floor to stand before the man.

He looked her over slowly, then leaned back on the bed, bracing his arms behind him and opening and extending his legs.

The girl knelt between his legs and slowly unbuttoned his worn blue work shirt, then slid it off his shoulders. It fell to the bed but he did not lift his hands to free himself of it. He closed his eyes and his head rolled backward.

For the first time since the door was opened, she was out of the man's direct gaze. For the first time, she hesitated.

And felt strong fingers grip her throat.

"Do it," the man rasped as he squeezed hard. The fingers hurt her.

"I will, I will. I'm tryin' to remember."

He squeezed tighter. "Do it now. Just like I told you."

She could hardly speak. She was almost choking. "I . . . I can't yet. I gotta remember."

The man pushed his hand up, under her chin. His knuckles popped her jawbone. The force clamped her mouth shut. Her teeth clicked loudly. He kept pushing. Her head whipped back; her neck ached. He lifted her to her feet and hurled her facedown onto the bed.

He threw himself onto her back. She coughed as her breath was unexpectedly and hurtfully squished from her lungs. Grabbing a handful of her brown hair, he yanked her head backward and hissed into her ear, "I'm payin' you good money, bitch. Better than you get anyplace else. Better than a piece like you is *worth*."

"Okay, okay," she gasped. "But I'm warnin' you, you hurt me this time and it will be your last, you bastard."

The man smiled a thin, spiteful smile. "Hurt you, babe? What are you talkin' about? What do you take me for? I like you, babe. I always ask for you special."

He relaxed his pull on her neck but he did not let go of her hair. Nor did he move his weight off her slim body. "Now do it, babe."

She sucked air into her lungs. "Let me up."

"Sure, babe, sure. In a minute. You do it first."

"I can't—"

He pulled her hair, flipping her head back. She winced with pain.

"*Do* it," he yelled in her ear.

"M-Mick, baby, you are so . . . beautiful. I . . . I want you, Mickey, baby. Bad. You're so strong." She tried to coo, to caress with her voice, but it was difficult. Her neck hurt so much. Her throat was almost closed off. It was hard to breathe. "You're so hard. You're everything a man should be."

The man took great pleasure in the words.

He loosened his grip a little.

Then the phone rang. He ignored it. It rang again.

"Don't stop *now*, bitch." He pulled her hair harder than before. The phone kept ringing.

She yelped, "I *can't*. The phone."

He pulled until her chest came off the bed. Then he giggled and pushed her down.

The phone was on a radiator, next to the bed. He grabbed at it. "Who the fuck is this?"

He listened. His face slowly drained of anger. He grinned slyly. "Well, now, how do? Nice to hear from you. Gettin' near my time to call you. But I like this. Maybe we'll keep it like this. What do you say?"

He listened again and his face went blank.

"That so? We'll have to do something about that, won't we?"

He listened once more, then hung up. For a moment he stared off into space. Then he turned back to the young girl on the bed. She had moved onto her side. She was breathing heavily and rubbing her neck.

He grinned at her. "Now, babe, where were we?"

Jenny worked on the unicorn. She had sanded it smooth, removing the faded, chipped paint. The wood was in remarkably good condition. She had only to fill a few nicks and scratches, sand and treat them, and then she could start painting. As she stripped and repaired the animal figures she also worked on a color scheme for each. She wanted every creature to be special and unique. Their colors should convey the energy and grace of their sculpture. Each one must be

vibrant and alive but at the same time they should blend
easily with one another. She wanted to create an overall effect
of bounding innocence. Of magnificent, elemental beings
frolicking with unchecked vigor and in unfettered freedom.
Benign creatures. Without pasts or futures. Frozen forever on
a revolving turntable, caught in a moment of untainted
simplicity and happiness.

She had looked for the tall, lean jogger and his crazy dog
on the way to work. But they had not been on the beach.
She'd been a little rough on him. Thinking about it later, she
had to laugh at her misunderstanding. And the dog was kind
of cute in a mischievous way. They were oddly matched but,
in some bizarre way, she thought, well suited.

Well, maybe she'd run into them again. Maybe not. No
matter.

She emptied her mind of thought and concentrated on her
work. She did not want to let her mind wander, for she knew
where it would lead. She must not think of it. She had
planned well and she had begun. It was well past the time for
debate and self-examination. She knew what she must do.
What she had waited all these years to do. What Elizabeth—

She was doing it. Thinking.

She returned to the unicorn.

Harry sat at his typewriter-table desk. He'd spent more time
in San Paulo than he'd thought he would. But there was no
leaving now. Things were just getting interesting. Hell of a
coincidence that another stiff turns up with his balls blown off
and his head punctured. Small world, isn't it?

But what could he do? He had no real authority down here.
And goddamned Jannings couldn't see beyond his bruised
pride and continent-sized ego. Hell, Harry thought, there was
nothing wrong with ego if you could back it up. If you could

deliver. But once it kept you from doing your job right and producing results, then it was time to swallow hard and bite the bullet. But how the hell was he going to make Jannings understand that? He could push the situation only so far, then Jannings would . . .

What the hell's the use of thinking about it? He'd do what he had to do and let happen what would happen. Jannings be damned.

He got up from the typewriter table and went to the nearest unoccupied real desk. He picked up the phone and dialed the San Francisco Police Department.

"Inspector King, please. Callahan calling."

He was put on hold. After a moment the line came alive and he heard rowdy baritone laughter.

"Horace, shut the hell up and listen. I need a favor. The ballistics report on the Wilburn killing. Get it to me, will you?"

"Sure thing, Harry. Hey, did you get him?"

"What? Oh. Yeah, I got him. He's almost as ugly as you. But he does have his good points."

Horace's voice took on a serious tone. "I heard you had visitors. Through unofficial channels, you might say. I'm workin' it, Harry. Callin' in a lot of favors. You cover your ass till I get this arranged."

"Yeah. Listen, wire the report first thing in the morning. Thanks."

Harry hung up and looked around the squad room. Bennett had mentioned that the john was downstairs. He wondered what else might be down there. Like the lab, for instance. He got up and headed for the stairwell.

As he crossed in front of Janning's office he stopped and looked into it. The chief was still absent. Harry wondered about something. Maybe it was a hell of a small world. He entered the police chief's office and walked directly to the wall where the family photos were hanging.

He looked closely at the graduation-party shot. He studied the faces of the chief's son's friends. The boy sitting on the hood of the hot rod looked familiar. He was a little thinner in the picture and a little less sullen, but there was no mistake.

Kruger.

Harry reached to the inside breast pocket of his sport coat and took out a small manila envelope. He rooted around in it for a moment and extracted what he sought. A small, square police mug shot. He held it close to the picture on the wall and compared it to the other three boys lounging against the car. One of them resembled the mug shot. But there was less flesh, more hair, and a whole lot more life.

The mug shot was of a dead man, lying on the floor of a car. A car parked in the parking lot of the Cliff House Restaurant.

They looked a little alike. But it was hard to tell conclusively.

Wilburn. Maybe.

He left the office, crossed to the stairwell, and walked to the basement. The johns were there, just as Bennett had said. And so was the lab. He pushed open the door.

An Oriental man was leaning over a microscope. He wore a long white lab coat and tortoiseshell reading glasses. When Harry entered, he looked up from his work without raising his head. He peered over the half-lens spectacles, looked him up and down, then returned to the microscope.

Harry walked to the table where the man sat.

"Excuse me, I'm—"

"I know who you are." The man kept his head down.

"Right." Harry glanced around. It was a modest lab but it seemed to have all the essentials. He wondered if there were other technicians on staff. The workload would be staggering for only one man. Unless he were damn good. But even then the paperwork would be enormous. "You finished the ballistics on the Kruger kill? I need a copy of the report."

"No, Inspector Callahan." He still did not look up from the microscope. "I haven't completed the report yet and, no, I can't let you have a copy."

"Look—"

"I can't help you." He finally looked up at Harry and sighed as he removed his glasses and started to massage the bridge of his nose. "Chief Jannings has given me a direct order." He looked a little tired or defeated. Or ashamed. "It means my job. I'm sorry."

Damn Jannings and his goddamned thickheaded pride. Why screw the case? Was he afraid he wouldn't get to pose for more pictures of more handshakes with more small-town big shots? Stupid shithead.

"Right."

Harry left the man to his work and walked back upstairs. He looked over to Jannings's office. The chief was still gone. Harry scanned the rest of the squad room. Bennett had come in. He was seated at his desk, typing.

Harry walked over and stood behind him. In a low voice he spoke to the young policeman without looking at him.

"I'll buy you a cup of coffee."

Bennett stopped typing. Before he could respond, Harry walked off in the direction of the coffee room.

Bennett sat and thought a moment. Then he opened a drawer of his desk and lifted out a San Francisco Forty-niners coffee mug.

He looked around to check on the curious eyes of his fellow officers, then casually got up from his desk, stretched, and went off toward the coffee room.

•   •   •

It was dark. The sun had set a few hours ago. Jenny had finished up her day's work at the carousel and biked home to its spectacular display of brilliant colors and reflections. The wind was strong and gusty. The bike ride had been a good workout. And just when she needed one. To rid her body of poisonous lactic acid. To drive away tensions and anxieties. To soothe and relax her. She had something important to do tonight and would have to be at her best. Things had gone well for her so far. Better than she had ever expected. She must make them go that way throughout.

The ocean was choppy and restive when she exited her house after a cleansing, priming shower and some strong tea. As she drove along West Cliff she drew on its strength and resolve as much as she could. She had to store it up. Tonight would be the first one away from the limitless expanse and depth of the sea. She'd be truly alone this time. She'd have nothing but her memory and her sorrow and her long-ago but undiminished pain to guide her. She knew it would be more than sufficient.

She sat in her gray Firenza, parked across and down from the hardware store on the corner. The moon was out. It was full and bright, and she could see very well the closed doors of the store. In just a few minutes they'd be locking those doors to service the last remaining customers inside and then tally the register. It was, generally, a rather quick procedure. Only one man was required to stay and complete it. The owner of the store. The man whose name was stenciled across each of the wide, high plate-glass windows on either side of the front doors.

How ironic, Jenny thought. One of them had succeeded. He was a businessman now. Owned his own home, in a brand-new development. Supporter of local civic groups. A functioning, contributing member of the community. An example to the youth of the town. What nonsense. What stupid, pitiful nonsense. It needed to be set right. It cried out for justice.

Justice. How could she ever—how could anyone ever—expect the justice that was due her? And Elizabeth? How could it be done? How could things ever be made right? She asked the question of herself now even though she had asked it countless times before. She knew the answer. It was absurdly simple. Things could not be made right. The brutal acts inflicted upon her and her sister had irrevocably altered their lives. They had smashed into these aberrations and been sent spinning in directions they would never have chosen. There was nothing she could do about that now except deal with and somehow manage the new course of their lives.

And that course included a pathetically unequal righting of wrong. A retribution.

Jenny checked her watch. It was time.

Her shoulder bag lay on the seat beside her. She picked it up, looped the strap over her arm, and opened the car door with a gloved hand.

She entered the store and started to move slowly about, pretending to browse. She was surprised that the place was so large and fully stocked. Business must be good. She walked along an aisle of electrical fixtures and searched the store for Tyrone.

She found him almost immediately, leading a customer from the carpentry section to the cash register. He was the picture of helpful, polite efficiency in his red-lettered blue smock. His sandy hair was brushed neatly and his face was clean shaven.

She remembered another version of this same face. But the hair was greasy and matted with sweat. The face was shadowed with a scraggly beard. She remembered it as it rolled off her sister, winded, satisfied. Gloating but still greedy to inflict pain.

This same but much less bourgeois face had whooped with glee. Had yelled with accomplishment and pride. Had bragged and demanded.

"Oh, yeah," the face had exclaimed. "That's the way. But don't forget, buddy boys, I got my turn at the other. Just gimme a second."

The face had laughed then, mirthlessly, ruthlessly.

It was joined by other laughter.

She remembered the roughness of the hands that clamped her own hands and feet, and held them still. That pressed her mouth and kept it quiet.

She remembered that she had never stopped fighting those hands.

And she remembered that Elizabeth had stopped. Stopped screaming and crying and struggling. She had stopped moving.

But they didn't stop. They kept at her.

This face's other version had then hovered over her own. It had blotted out one abhorrent vision and had become the central character in another.

This face. Different but the same.

"We're closing in five minutes, folks."

Jenny looked over to see a young blue-smocked clerk walk to the door, opened it, and usher out two older ladies. He closed the door behind him and locked it. Then he flipped over the *open* sign so that it read *closed*.

She noted that there were still three other customers in the store. One was at the register; two were still selecting their purchases.

Jenny walked softly to the back of the store and searched for a place where she could conceal herself. She was careful to keep out of the sight of the clerks and the customers. She did not have to worry about Tyrone. He was at the register, giving his full attention to the transaction at hand. Conscientious and courteous. A model merchant.

She came to a door at the rear of the store, adjacent to the back room; LAVATORY was stenciled on it in black block letters. How discreet.

Jenny opened the door and stepped into the small cubicle. There was a toilet and a sink with a square wall mirror about it.

Jenny closed the door.

She'd wait.

Two female clerks sat at the round table in the coffee room, finishing the last of some home-baked chocolate-chip cookies and the remaining few minutes of their afternoon break. It seemed to Harry that their conversation got a lot quieter when he entered the area. And they didn't offer him any of the cookies. That was a damn shame. They looked pretty good. The kind with lots of chunks of pecans. He was a little hungry but the stale-looking junk in the machines in the coffee room was totally unappetizing. He'd wait till he got out of the squad room and maybe head over to that Oceana Mall, check out the restaurants there. Maybe find a good chocolate-chip-cookie store.

Where the hell was Bennett? He was a nice kid but a nervous sort. He had the makings, though, Harry thought. But he'd have to decide for himself which way he was going to go. Follow things through, dog them to the end. Make waves and bother people. But get the job done the best way he knew how. Regardless of the fallout. Or coast along. Roll with the punches. Look the other way. Put in the time and make the brass nod their approval. Every cop had to choose at one point or another. Some guys had to keep making the choice over and over.

Bennett couldn't have been on the force too long. He looked as if he'd just got home from the junior prom. Maybe he was a rookie. One thing was sure, though. He was going to get his chance to choose right away. Right now, as a matter of fact. If he'd ever leave his desk.

One of the clerks was doing her damnedest to peek at Harry unobtrusively. He poured himself some coffee from the automatic drip that was constantly in use and offered her some. That flustered her. She shook her head to refuse, blushed pink, snatched a cookie from its plastic container, and bit into it. She was a tad too forceful, however, and the cookie crumbled onto her chest and lap.

Bennett finally arrived. He was about to speak but didn't when he saw the two clerks.

Harry poured him some coffee from the pot he still held. "So, Officer Bennett, you a Forty-niners fan?"

Bennett looked at him, puzzled. "What?"

Harry nodded at the coffee mug and then the clerks.

"Oh." The cop caught on. "Yes, sir. Love the 'Niners. I try to get up to the city for at least one game a season. Yeah, that Super Bowl trophy is bound for the 'Niners' locker room. If not this year, then bet on next."

The kid was overdoing it but the women didn't seem to notice. They cleared their places and left the room.

Harry got right to the point.

"You know the pictures hanging on Jannings's wall? The family stuff with his kid?"

Bennett nodded.

"I want you to find out about the people in the hot-rod shot."

The young cop put down his coffee. "Inspector, I owe

you . . . a lot. And I like . . . I admire the way you handle yourself. You're not like any cops I've known. I'd like to help you. I really would. But do you have any idea what you're asking?''

"I'm asking a fellow police officer to assist in the investigation of two homicides that appear, more and more, to be connected.''

The words hit Bennett like a slap.

"Okay. But, Jesus, if Chief Jannings finds out—''

"He won't. Just try to get the information as best you can. Their names, where they live, where they work.''

"It's not going to be easy, Inspector.''

"What the hell is?''

"I don't dare take that picture off the wall. How am I going to ID those people and trace them without their pictures?''

Time to hold class, Harry thought.

"It's a graduation photo, right? Find out what high school Jannings's kid attended. Then go there and check out the annual for the year he got out.''

"Allright.'' Bennett would do it but he wouldn't like it much. That didn't matter. Liking it didn't count. Doing did.

Bennett picked up his coffee mug and started to leave.

"One more thing,'' Harry told him. "I want to see Kruger's sheet.''

Bennett was starting to look overwhelmed. "Anything else?''

"Yeah. His address. I'll need it right away.

Jenny checked her watch. It was dark in the closet-sized room but she couldn't risk turning on the light because she wasn't sure if the exhaust fan was hooked into the same circuit. In most store bathrooms it was usually that way. She didn't need to take the chance, however, because her watch face was luminous.

It had been almost twenty minutes. Long enough. She wanted out of the tiny black space. She wanted it over with.

She cracked the door carefully. It made no sound. A long sliver of light cut into the cramped washroom. Jenny put her eye close to the narrow slit and surveyed what she could of the store. She saw no one. She opened the door a fraction more and turned her head so that her ear was pressed against the opening. She listened. At first she heard nothing at all. Then she heard the register. It was an old NCR model and it required a good deal of time and key punching to close out its final reading. It also made quite a bit of noise. She heard that noise now. Just starting up. That meant Tyrone would be alone and his attention would be thoroughly taken by the tabulation of the day's profits.

It was time to make her move.

As she opened the lavatory door just wide enough to slip her narrow body through, she caught sight of herself in the square wall mirror above the washbasin. She saw her face. Her eyes.

She stared at herself. The reflected image she saw wore a blank, expressionless face. The jaw, the lips, the cheeks, the nostrils, the eyebrows, and forehead. All were in repose. No signs of stress or tension. No physically tangible signals of worry or fear or anxiety. All her features were calm and serene.

Except her eyes.

There was something different about them. Something she had never seen before.

They were implacable. Feral.

She stepped out of the lavatory and moved slowly and silently past the tools and the nails and the house paints and the bolts and the washers and the hoses to the front of the store. When she turned the corner of the electrical-equipment aisle, she saw the back of a light blue smock and the back of a sandy-haired head.

She left the concealment of a shelving unit and walked out into the open area in front of the main counter and the cash register.

Tyrone was counting the change drawer. The NCR was churning away.

She reached into her shoulder bag.

Tyrone dropped some coins. He bent to pick them up off the floor.

The register ceased its din.

Tyrone turned his head as he retrieved a coin.

She tightened her hold on the gun grip.

He saw her.

She looked at his face.

It wasn't Tyrone.

"Miss . . . we're closed." It was a clerk. She hadn't seen him before. He was the same height, the same build. The smock . . . the hair . . . "Couple more minutes and you'd been locked in for the night. Can I help you with something?"

She had almost . . . She took her hand from the bag.

"No. I'll come back." She went straight for the door.

He hurried around the counter. "Hold on. I gotta open it for you."

She waited as he unlocked and opened the door.

"Thank you." She exited the store and walked quickly to her car.

"Come back tomorrow, now," he called after her, eager to please, anxious to avoid the loss of a sale.

She climbed into her Oldsmobile and slammed the door closed. She wasn't ready to drive. She sat there a moment.

She realized she'd been holding her breath since she left the clerk. She exhaled slowly. She raised her hands. They weren't shaking. But her heart was beating hard and fast.

She'd come very close.

To killing the wrong man. An innocent man. Innocent, at least, of the crime with which she was concerned.

And to revealing herself. The gun was almost out of the bag when he'd looked up to see her. What would she have done then?

And which was worse? Which would have harmed her more?

Which "almost" was making her heart race?

Which one would she have regretted?

She reached into her jacket pocket for her keys and started the car. As she looked for oncoming traffic she saw her face in the rearview mirror.

Her eyes.

She studied them.

11

Harry turned onto the San Paulo Pier and drove out as far as traffic was allowed. He left his car and walked out toward the end of the structure, looking for Kruger's Fish and Live Bait.

He found it beside a pretty good-looking restaurant. It was the last building on the pier and fairly large. The odor of fish was already in the air, but it got even stronger as he approached the market.

It was close to nine o'clock but the full moon gave off plenty of light. The pier was empty of fishermen but there were quite a few couples out strolling. There was a short line outside the restaurant, composed mostly of large families.

Kruger had living quarters above the fish market, but Harry found the place still open for business. He stepped up to a long glass-and-chrome refrigerator case and saw a thin, frumpy woman sitting in a beach chair in the far corner of the space. Her frizzy brown hair was parted in the middle and pulled into a carelessly packed bun on the back of her head. She

wore an old granny dress over thick boots, a frayed flight
jacket zippered to her throat, and a long rubber apron. Her
expression was morose.

Off to the other side of the market two men worked,
cleaning and filleting fish. They, too, were bundled against
the strong sea breezes. One wore a bulky sweater, the other a
weathered leather jacket. Each had a woolen watch cap pulled
low on his forehead. Both men also wore rubber aprons. But
theirs were reddened with bloodstains. They were sturdily
built. Broad shoulders, thick legs. One was of medium
height, about five ten, but the other guy was huge. Taller than
Harry. Had to be at least six six, he figured.

He looked at their hands as they worked, one with a long
knife, the other with a cleaver. Although they both had large,
thick-fingered hands, they wielded the tools of their trade
nimbly. Harry watched them chop and slice dead fish. Very
nimbly.

Harry turned to the woman. "Excuse me. Mrs. Kruger?"

She looked at him but didn't speak.

"Could I talk with you?"

She scowled at him. The men stopped chopping and
slicing, and glared at him. The shorter man wore a bushy
black beard. He stepped forward. "You from the insurance
company, pal?"

Harry noted that he still held the cleaver. Drops of blood
were dripping from it and disappearing as they hit the
sawdust-covered floor.

"No. I'm—"

"Then unless you want to buy fish or bait, get your ass out
of here."

Nice friendly bunch, Harry thought. The big guy put down
his knife and stepped forward, too.

Harry looked back at the woman. "Mrs. Kruger, my name is Callahan—"

"You got shit in your ears, buddy?" The big guy was getting rammy. He had a thick black handlebar mustache on his upper lip, which he jutted out at Harry. Daring him to be flip.

Harry tried the woman one more time. "Mrs. Kruger, I want to ask you some questions."

The two hulks moved forward.

"About your late husband."

The men flanked him now, but were restrained from any aggressive action at that moment by a long, high-pitched wail that turned into a roar. The woman came off her seat and assumed a wrestler's ready position.

"That lousy son of a bitch," she yelled. "He leaves me nothing. Not a crummy thing. I got bills up to my ass. He lets the goddamned insurance run out. And then he gets killed whackin' off to dirty pictures. When he ain't touched me in months, that bastard—" Her anger erupted so fully that it cut off her words. She shook her fists grimly at the inside of the market, as though her husband or his spirit were still there.

The shorter man tapped the flat side of the cleaver against his other palm. "Our sister's in mourning, asshole. Now get the fuck out of here."

Harry had had enough of these clowns.

"Why don't you boys go suck on some fish heads."

They came at him.

They were already close to him but each took a giant step forward for leverage. The one to swing back the cleaver, the other to pull back his log of an arm for a roundhouser. They were quick but Harry was a whole lot quicker.

He stomped his heel hard onto the toes of the cleaver carrier. Even through the guy's work shoe he could feel the toes splay out. At the same time, he used his left hand to help drive his right elbow into the big brother's gut. Both men doubled over.

Harry then slammed the heel of his right hand into the bridge of the cleaver man's nose. Blood sprayed out as the man flew back onto a large metal drum filled with fish innards and crashed it to the floor. He was instantly inundated with fish guts.

While the cleaver guy was falling, Harry very quickly rammed his left knee into the other brother's face. The huge man stumbled backward, his arms flailing for balance, which he did not find. His falling body smashed through the glass-and-chrome refrigerator case.

Harry turned to the woman.

She was aiming a rifle at him.

"I'll come back," he said, "when you're less bereaved."

It was a short walk back to the car and a short drive along Beach Street to La Bahía. His interview with the grieving widow and her consoling brothers had gotten him nothing but a little exercise, and that had made him even hungrier than he was when he'd left the station. Maybe Bennett would come up with something, some common thread that he could follow. Or maybe Jannings would come to his senses and take the chip off his shoulder. In any event, there was nothing left to do tonight but get a good meal, take Pissface for his walk, and then grab some sack time.

Harry changed into brown corduroys, a long-sleeved navy-blue pullover, and running shoes. He strapped on his shoulder holster and put on a gray windbreaker over it. Pissface was waiting at the door as he finished.

After a short tour of the beach, where the dog attended to

his duties, they piled into the car and drove toward midtown San Paulo.

Harry parked on Jackson street and he and Pissface walked over to the Oceana Mall. The night had gotten much cooler and some fog had begun to roll into the town. Even so, there were quite a few people on the street. Harry and Pissface walked along.

There was an odd assortment of browsers and strollers who reflected the mixed group that combined to make up the town. Although it was rather late, a lot of the stores were still open. Evidently, the foot traffic was heavy enough, even off season, to merit the long hours. There were plenty of posh stores along the street, selling all kinds of things, but Harry wasn't interested in them. He was appraising the restaurants.

He and Pissface were approaching the end of a block when he heard music. Jazz. Not bad, either. He walked up to the corner to investigate and found Neale's, a three-story brownstone-and-brick building. The interior was a conglomeration of stores and booths and boutiques. The basement was a steak-and-chop charcoal-burning restaurant. The front of the building had been sectioned off from the street by black cast-iron grillwork, and a sidewalk café had been set up in the space between.

The café ran the length of the building. A five-piece combo was making its music at one end. At the other end, near the corner, Harry spotted the blonde cyclist from the beach. She was sitting alone, sipping a glass of white wine.

He watched her a moment and then she saw him.

Their eyes held on each other.

Then Harry looked down at Pissface and pointed to the ground. The dog settled himself immediately. Harry looked back at the young woman. She raised her eyebrows in mock surprise, then nodded in approval.

Well, now, Harry thought, that was one of the few times in the last week or so that somebody'd acknowledged his presence without trying to shoot him, cut him, run him over, or chew him out. What the hell, he figured, he was on a roll. Why not ride it out?

He entered the café and walked to her table as the musicians finished their set and announced a short break.

"You've come a long way," she said, sipping her wine.

"Yeah, well, somebody told me to get it together."

She smiled. "Somehow I get the feeling you've heard that before."

Harry made no reply. He looked at her.

She looked right back.

"I may have been a little gruff the other day," she said, fingering the rim of the glass. "You and . . . your friend caught me unawares. If I was, I'm sorry."

Harry thought it over. What the hell.

"Buy me a beer and we'll call us even."

Now she thought it over.

"Okay."

She beckoned to a waiter as Harry sat down at the table. The waiter came over quickly.

"A beer for Mr. . . . ."

"Callahan. Harry Callahan."

"And one more of these for me, please." She tapped her wineglass lightly.

The waiter left them. They sat quietly for a few seconds. Then she extended a small white hand. "I'm Jenny Spenser."

Harry shook her hand. It was warm. They sat looking at each other until the waiter served their drinks.

"How's the police business?" she asked.

Harry poured himself some beer. "You think I'm a cop?"

"I saw you out here in the street the other day. I also saw

the commotion this morning in front of the Bahía Hotel. You're either a cop or public enemy number one.''

Harry drank some beer. ''Some might say both.''

''Really? Who?''

''Bozos with big brass nameplates on their desks and asses shaped like the seats of their chairs.'' He drank some more beer.

She smiled again. Almost laughed. ''Why?''

Harry put down his glass. ''You really want to know?'' She nodded.

''A question of methods. People want results but they don't want to do what has to be done to get them.''

Harry saw the young woman's face change.

''And you do?''

''I do what I have to do.''

''Good. I'm glad, Mr. Callahan. But, you know, you're an endangered species. This is an age of lapsed responsibilities and defeated justice. Today we interpret an eye for an eye to mean only if you're caught, and even then it's indefinite postponement and let's settle out of court.'

She sipped her wine.

''Did that sound profound? Or just boring? I'm sorry. I'm sure you hear that sort of thing all the time.''

''No. I don't hear it enough.''

She smiled again. But this time brighter, more open. ''Well, I promise to adjourn Philosophy one-oh-one.''

''What do you do?''

''I paint.''

''Yeah? Houses? Cars?'

''Horses.''

Harry was lifting his glass. He stopped and eyed her over it.

''Hobbyhorses. I'm restoring the carousel.''

He drank his beer. She drank more wine.

"Somehow, Mr. Callahan—"

"Harry."

"Okay. Somehow, Harry, you don't seem the typical San Paulo police officer."

"I'm not."

"Typical?"

"San Paulo policeman. I'm with the San Francisco department. Homicide."

"Don't tell me this is your idea of a vacation."

"I'm working. A case needed background."

They had both finished their drinks. Harry looked around for the waiter. When he got his attention, he signaled for another round.

"Anything interesting?" she asked him.

"It's developing."

"Any theories?"

The waiter took away their empty glasses and Harry's beer bottle, and served them fresh drinks.

"Somebody's started killing," Harry told her. "I got a feeling it's going to go on for a while."

"A psycho?"

"Maybe. Or maybe somebody's paying back some old debt."

"Revenge."

"It's one of the oldest and strongest motives for action there is."

"But you don't approve."

"Revenge is fine. Until it breaks the law."

The quintet resumed playing. Harry and Jenny listened awhile and finished their drinks.

"Another?" Harry asked as she put down her glass.

"No," she said, shaking her head. "I work early.'

She reached into her shoulder bag, which hung beside her on the arm of the chair. Cued by her movement, Harry reached for his wallet.

"I'll get it," he said.

"No way," she countered. "A deal's a deal." She laid some bills on the table and placed her empty wineglass on top of them. Then she unlooped her bag from the chair and stood. Harry stood, too, and stepped aside to let her pass. He followed her to the front of the café.

The combo was playing a quick up-tempo number as they exited the wrought-iron canopy that framed the entrance to the café. The saxophone player ventured away from the ordered course of the song and began to weave an improvisation against the steady beat of the drums and the bass. Fog had blown in on a growing night breeze. The street was much grayer and cooler than before. A small congregation of people had formed on the sidewalk in front of the café. They were mostly couples and they were smiling kindly at the object of their attention.

Harry and Jenny saw an old woman at the center of a three-quarter circle of spectators. She was dressed in a sort of clown's or mummer's costume. She wore a long-sleeved blousy top and puffy full-length pantaloons. The neck, wrists, and ankles of her outfit were gathered snugly about her and fringed with long frilly material. She wore a floppy cap that was also frilled, and canvas high-top basketball sneakers. She was striped in bold, vivid purple and yellow and red and blue and green and orange. Her face was colored over with clown-white greasepaint, and her cheeks, forehead, nose, and lips were highlighted with the bright colors of her costume. She waved a striped, long-necked parasol high above her head as she improvised a strutting, pirouetting, sashaying dance.

Jenny joined the circle of admirers and smiled widely as she observed the unique performance. Harry followed and stood behind her. The old lady frequently broke her routine to approach the watchers and attempt to cajole them into joining her in a makeshift dance. Some people gave in to her silent coaxing and danced. Others did not.

The woman spotted Jenny and went right to her. Seeing Harry, she tried to persuade them both to dance. Jenny refused her gently but the woman persisted. Soon the whole crowd was looking. The woman took Jenny's hand and tried to nudge her forward. Still refusing, Jenny moved a few steps into the circle. The woman then clasped one of Harry's hands and pulled. He did not budge. A few members of the crowd began to clap and urge the woman on. The woman turned back to Jenny with a clown's baleful, pleading expression. Jenny was shaking her head in an exaggerated mime of refusal when the music changed. Led by the saxophone, the other instruments slowed down and wound a melancholy way around the tune's original path.

The mummer lady looped an arm around Harry's waist and extended one of Jenny's arms. They now formed a three-person dance team. The lady tried to ease them into a little two-step but they were adamant. She finally surrendered to their reluctance and moved on to another couple. But as she left them she guided Jenny close to Harry, looping one of their arms around the other's waist. She then lifted one of Harry's hands to support Jenny's extended arm.

When she saw that they were joined closely together, she smiled a sentimental clown's smile and left them.

Jenny and Harry, their arms around each other in the classic slow dancers' pose, did not dance. For a moment they just stood there, Harry towering over her, and looked at each other.

Jenny then slipped her hand out of Harry's and withdrew her arm from around his waist.

"Well . . . good night."

Jenny left him. He watched her walk away into the gray night. He kept watching even after she had disappeared into the darkness. A waiter's voice finally distracted him.

"Mister, that your dog?"

Harry turned to see the waiter standing at his side. "Why, you want him?"

The waiter looked puzzled, then pointed to the far end of the café.

Harry looked in the direction of the young man's gesture and saw Pissface standing by some flower pots that lined the café's wall of elaborate grillwork. The dog's leg was lifted high over the pots. Three young women seated at a table directly on the other side of the grille scurried out of their chairs as Pissface let loose with a strong, steady, hissing stream.

The waiter looked at Harry.

Harry mumbled to himself, "Swell."

An hour later, Jenny was at home. She had changed into her nightgown and gone to bed, but she could not fall asleep. She'd succeeded in clearing her mind of conscious thought, but still she could not relax. Faces kept appearing to her. Not the cruel, smirking animal faces that had haunted her dreams for years after the torture night. She had, by a single, prodigious, bludgeoning act of will, banished their unbidden ugliness from her nights forever. Other faces appeared to her now. The face of the clerk at the hardware store. Elizabeth's face. And the face of the cop from San Francisco. He was a homicide detective, collecting data, researching a murder case. What case? There could be no other. And now a second killing had occurred. An unmistakable connection would be made. What would this cop do? He looked like the stubborn type. A good cop. One who saw. One who did not turn away. Yet, even so, he would—could—never understand. What irony, she thought. Years, too many years, too late.

She got out of bed, put on her robe, and went to the living room. She slid open one side of her window wall and did not mind the cold sea air that rushed in to engulf her. The wind was still brisk, the sea still choppy. She could hear the waves crashing on the rocks below.

The moon bounced its own reflected light off the water and into Jenny's house. She could see the work-in-progress resting on its easel on the other side of the room. She crossed to it. Much had been done. Jenny folded her arms tightly over her breasts as she gazed at it.

A head had taken clear shape. Hair swirled out from it. A face was not so clear but easily discerned. The lines and colors on the canvas were dead, still things. But, joined together, crossed and curved and blended into one another, they took on a life of their own. They moved and swelled and roiled. Eye sockets had been shaped but not filled. Yet, even so, there was a depth, a bottomless, penetrating, scrutinizing endlessness to them. Lips were sketched and colorless, yet they were taut and pulled back to scream silently. A chin that was only a thin line was thrust out in stretched anxiety and crackling tension. Strokes of red and black, purple and gray, and dark burnt orange swept up, straining to burst free of the surface of the portrait.

Jenny turned from the canvas and studied the image of her face in the mirror beside the painting. She examined the smooth, soft rounding of her lips and chin. She studied her eyes.

After a time she reached over to a small bureau that she was using as a workbench and lifted a brush.

Harry and Pissface were returning from a last, short walk on the beach. They were both well fed and ready for sleep. Harry had gone into the Neale's building and had a good, rare steak, a baked potato, and salad. Actually, he'd ordered two steaks. One to go. Besides being a royal and embarassing pain in the ass, Pissface was becoming a drain on his wallet.

They crossed Beach Street and walked up toward La Bahía. The fog was a thick, wet gray curtain that considerably shortened visibility, and the rough breakers filled the night air with crashing wave sounds. Even so, Harry stopped abruptly and scanned the street ahead of him. The dog stopped, too, and focused on the same area.

Harry thought he could hear someone walking slowly toward him from the opposite end of the street. He listened even more intensely, not only for the suspected sound in front of him but also for possible sounds approaching him from the side or rear. He heard none of these. Only ahead of him. There was someone coming at him. Slowly, deliberately.

He unzipped his windbreaker and reached under his arm to withdraw the Magnum. He dropped his arm to his side and angled the weapon behind his leg.

Horace might be working on it, he thought, but he sure in hell hadn't fixed it. Two teams sent out. Two teams terminated. But punks grew on trees. With Threlkiss down, there must be a hell of a lot of husky cigar lighters and champagne pourers and chair movers with nothing to do. Well, Harry would do whatever he could to help them solve their problem. Too much time on their hands? He could take care of that real easy. He could—

A shape was taking form in the shadowy gray in front of

him. A man shape. It was moving out of the fog and coming straight at him. Its head was slightly bowed, its shoulders stooped. It walked slowly, dragging its feet slightly with every step. A rumpled golf cap was pulled low on its head.

Harry lightly flexed his hand and fingers around the grip of his weapon. One finger, however, did not move at all. It hugged the trigger of the powerful handgun, applying a slight, constant pressure.

The man shape stopped walking. It lifted its head and squared its shoulders. It was cleanly outlined against a gray background of fog.

Harry watched it, listening for other sounds of movement from other directions. There were still none.

The man shape started to walk again. It came close. Harry could see its wrinkled, mottled, blue-veined face clearly.

It was an old man.

He nodded at Harry and kept on walking, his shoulders and head stooped again.

Harry watched him pass. He waited. Nothing happened. The old man kept dragging his feet. Soon he was swallowed up by the mist and the gray. Soon there was no sound of his steps.

An old man. Out for a midnight stroll.

Crazy bastard, Harry thought, and smiled a little. He could get himself killed.

Harry holstered the Magnum and led Pissface to their hotel.

12

Jenny slipped on her soft gloves as she sat in her car outside
Tyrone's house. She'd been waiting since just after dawn.
There would be no mistakes this time, no near catastrophes.
Tyrone lived alone in a partially occupied development of
tract homes on the northwestern outskirts of San Paulo. His
upwardly mobile status had allowed him to purchase a corner
property that consisted of a slightly larger-than-average two-
story house and an adjoining two-car garage. His lawn was
not yet completely sodded, his hedges and shade trees not yet
fully landscaped. Newspaper was substituting for curtains and
drapes, but Jenny could visualize his card table, folding-chair
dining-room set, and his sleeping-bag bedroom decor. All in
good time. No need to rush into purchases. A man's first
home required patient effort. His furnishings would help to
describe and define him to his friends and business associates. Tyrone was a solid member of the town's merchant
community. He must take time to pick and choose carefully.

147

He wouldn't want to give a wrong impression. Or create a less-than-flattering image. After all, he had something to lose now. Position. Possessions. A good name. Everything he'd worked for. The fulfillment of his own personal version of the American Dream.

Yes, Jenny thought, Tyrone had a lot to lose.

The motorized door of the garage began noisily to crank itself upward and inward. Jenny quickly checked the streets of the development. It was not quite seven-thirty. Papers had been delivered. No one was yet on his way to work. The nearest occupied house was well down the lane from Tyrone's house. And there were no morning walkers or joggers in sight. Conditions were perfect. There would be no mistakes, no unforeseen problems this time.

Her bag already hung from her shoulder. She slipped out of her car, carefully closing the door so as not to disturb the morning quiet, and hurried to the side of the house.

From the cover of the garage's front corner, she looked in to see Tyrone enter his car, a year-old Buick Riviera, and start its engine. She felt a rush of adrenaline pump so strongly through her that she nearly swayed. He was getting away. He was escaping her once more.

She was trying to decide whether to run back to her car or hide behind the house when she heard the engine cut off. She peered around the edge of the garage doorway to see Tyrone exit his car and go toward a stack of boxes piled at the back wall. He pushed and pulled and shifted boxes until he dragged out a long narrow footlocker from the bottom of the heap. Taking a jangling key ring from his pocket, he searched for the right key and opened the locker.

As he knelt and rooted inside it, Jenny slipped into the garage and, clinging to the shadows of a side wall, advanced very slowly toward the rear wall and Tyrone. She saw Tyrone find what he was looking for, an old Army-issue automatic. He dug out a clip, checked it, and loaded the gun. He stood and shoved the gun inside the waistband of his trousers.

As he turned to return to his car Jenny eased her hand into her bag and gripped her weapon tightly. Then she stepped out of the shadows to face him.

Tyrone froze when he saw her. His eyes bulged wide. His fair-skinned face was drained of what little color it had. He stared intently at her face as if he were altering her features to compare her to another face buried deep in his memory. The process was very quick. In a second he knew. Without doubt. Without question. She was here. In front of him. In his very own garage.

His eyes lost their shocked, bulging openness and squeezed to a half-lidded, devious hopefulness. He grabbed at his waist for his gun. Jenny was much quicker. In an instant her revolver was out of her shoulder bag and pointing at Tyrone. Her feet were set in a shooter's stance, her arms extended fully before her. She held the gun steady with both hands.

He abruptly stopped his move for his gun. His hand hung in the air. His eyes lost their sly hope as he looked into the barrel of the shiny .38. He was very close to fear.

With a flick of her gun Jenny ordered him to return his hand to his side. He did.

"The witch was right," he said in a low, breathy voice. "It is you."

Jenny stepped closer to him.

His eyes shifted and bobbed in their sockets. He was afraid. Dreadfully afraid. But he was thinking fast. Scheming. There had to be a way for him. He had to find it.

"Look, you got to understand." He lifted and spread his arms wide in front of him. "It was a long time ago." He took a small, halting step forward. "More than ten years. I was a kid. A crazy kid. I didn't know anything. I was stupid. An idiot." He took another tiny tentative step toward her. "Hey, look, I know it was wrong. It was awful. But I didn't mean anything by it. I was drunk. Blind, lousy, out-of-my-skull drunk. I didn't know what the hell I was doing." His arms were moving nervously up and down and side to side in front of him. "I'm a businessman now. I'm making good money. Hey, I could let you have some. You need money, right? Hell, everybody does. So, tell me, how much do you want?"

He began to lift his foot for one more step.

Jenny cocked the .38.

His foot stopped.

His eyes went wild with panic and desperation.

He dropped to his knees. His hands flew up together before him in supplication. He begged, "Please, please don't do it. I'll give you every cent. Everything I own. The house, the car, the store. It wasn't my fault. Really. Believe me. Please believe me. It was the others. The others made me do it. They did. Please. Please . . ."

He covered his face with his hands and started to rub his skin. His neck and ears were flushed scarlet. He started to sob.

Jenny witnessed this gutless display with utter distaste. Her face was devoid of expression. Her hands were steady.

Tyrone uncovered his face. His fingers had left rough red impressions. Tears streaked his cheeks. Mewling and panting, he pleaded with her. "It wasn't so bad, was it? Not bad enough to kill me for. People sell it, give it away free every day. Don't do this," he moaned. "Please don't shoot me."

Suddenly his sniveling and imploring stopped. He jumped to his feet and leaped at Jenny.

She lowered her aim and fired.

The bullet took him in mid-leap and at the crotch. He grabbed himself and thudded to the cold, damp cement floor.

His eyes were so surprised.

Jenny stepped close to him and fired once more.

The eyes twitched, lost all expressiveness, and became glazed in a blank, nonseeing, infinite stare.

Harry walked out of La Bahía's dim gloominess and into a bright, almost blinding sunshiny morning. The ocean was a smooth light blue that stretched out to met the nearly identical blue of the horizon. The sky was cloudless and the cresting breakers were bubbling their white foamy reach to the sand.

He looked over at the amusement area. A maintenance crew was just beginning their morning shift. Even though the summer crowds were gone, a good number of people still wanted to ride the rides and break the balloons to win a stuffed bear or cat. And, of course, they still put away the corn dogs and cotton candy and soda pop. And dropped the remains up and down the length of the boardwalk. Cleanup men were sticking and picking discarded waxed papers and Styrofoam cups, sweeping and hosing and emptying trash barrels. Work crews were starting to inspect and service individual amusement rides.

A few joggers were warming up on the sand and a couple of cyclists coasted slowly along Beach Street.

Neither one of them, though, was the blonde, pretty, oddly interesting Jenny Spenser.

Harry put on his sunglasses and walked to his car.

A few minutes later, he pulled into the San Paulo PD parking lot and headed for the station. Once inside the squad room, he made straight for his "desk." He checked to see if Bennett had arrived. He had.

Harry wanted to do something today. Shake the case up a

little. Get it moving. Maybe Horace's relay of the ballistics on Wilburn would knock the chip off Janning's shoulder and get him down to facts. Harry wouldn't have the Kruger ballistics report, but he figured he really didn't need it. He knew in his gut they'd match. No way they wouldn't. He could have used Bennett to smuggle him a copy of the findings, but he didn't want to push him too far. The young cop was already laying it on the line and taking some chances with his career. Harry didn't want to get Bennett screwed and, besides, the kid had plenty to work on already. Harry was very curious about the people in the picture.

A computer terminal chattered to life and began to punch out a fact sheet. Harry crossed the room and arrived at the machine at the same time as one of the department's female clerks. He bent over the computer and watched it print out. The clerk watched him. Feeling her stare, he turned to her. "Good morning," he said, not smiling.

"Good morning, Inspector Callahan," she answered, beaming.

"Got any chocolate-chip cookies today?" he asked.

"What?" Her happiness became confusion.

"Never mind." He went back to reading the printout. She looked at it for the first time. "Hey," she said, surprised. "This is for you."

"I know," he said. "I'm psychic."

The machine stopped its gibbering. Harry tore off the printout and read it once again.

"Something interesting, Inspector?" the clerk asked.

"Very," Harry told her, and walked off in the direction of Bennett's desk. He did not look at the young officer but tapped the top of his desk with the knuckle of his index finger as he passed by. Then, still reading the sheet, he went to the hallway and walked toward the coffee room.

Bennett looked around at the officers and clerks in the squad room. When he was certain that no one was looking his way, he lifted his desk blotter and slid out two sheets of paper from under it. He folded them over, twice, then opened his desk drawer, grabbed his coffee mug, and made for the coffee room.

Harry was standing by the coffee maker, stirring his coffee with a plastic straw. Bennett entered and walked straight to the coffee counter. Standing beside Harry, he set down his mug and the papers, and poured himself a cup of coffee. He reached for sugar and quickly glanced around the room. A cop was reading the sports section of the San Francisco *Chronicle* and a female clerk was reading a book. Bennett sugared his coffee and muttered to Harry as he returned the bowl to its place on the counter. "Wilburn was one of the group. So was Kruger."

He picked up his coffee mug and left the room.

Harry sipped his own coffee and eased his hand over the folded sheets Bennett had left behind. Turning his back to the other people in the room, he unfolded the pages and quickly scanned them.

Well, now, he thought, maybe things were beginning to lay out.

He refolded the sheets and pocketed them. He did the same with the printout. He sipped his coffee once more and grimaced. Rank stuff. Dropping the Styrofoam cup and its contents into a wastebasket, he left the room.

He crossed the squad room and was on his way to the front door when he heard a bellowing command. "Callahan. Get your ass in here."

All activity in the room ceased. All eyes were on him. Harry looked over to see Jannings standing in the doorway of his office. His hands were on his hips and his jaw jutted forward. He glared at Harry for a long few seconds, then turned his back. Harry watched him circle around his desk and seat himself, folding his hands in front of him on the desk top.

Harry took his time as he recrossed the squad room and entered Jannings's office.

"Shut the door," the police chief ordered in a firm, tense voice.

Harry shut the door.

"Sit down." Jannings seemed to struggle with himself momentarily. Harry thought he would lose the struggle and start yelling, but Jannings proved him wrong. He shifted into a more relaxed position in his chair and won control of himself.

Harry sat down in a straight-backed wooden chair in front of Jannings's desk. He waited for the police chief to speak. Jannings didn't. He just sat there.

Harry didn't know what the game was but he resolved not to lose it to Jannings. He leaned back in his chair and stared at the police chief. Jannings stared back.

Both men sat, silent and glaring, for almost two minutes, then Jannings's phone rang. Neither man looked at it or reached for it. It rang again. Jannings unfolded his hands.

"Pick it up," Jannings said when it rang a third time. "It's for you."

Now, what the hell's going on here? Harry thought as he lifted the receiver.

"Yeah?" His eyes wandered over to the wall of personal pictures as he spoke into the phone.

"Harry? Harry, is that you?" It was Lieutenant Donnelly. Harry did not answer him immediately. His attention had been taken by the photographs on the wall. One was missing.

Frame and all. There was only empty, faded wall in the space where the photo had been.

"Harry?" Donnelly was getting frantic.

Harry knew immediately which picture had been taken down. The graduation shot. The group.

"Damn it, Callahan." Donnelly was shouting.

"Yes, Lieutenant," Harry said into the phone's mouthpiece.

"Harry? What the hell is going on down there? It's supposed to be a research assignment, god damn it. Nothing else. Jannings has been bending the commissioner's ear. He's a good man. Go easy with him, will you? You don't have a hell of a lot of friends upstairs, Harry. Don't screw yourself. Okay? Understand?"

Harry looked away from the wall and back at Jannings. The chief hadn't taken his eyes off him.

"No," Harry answered Donnelly. "I don't understand. At all."

Before his lieutenant could respond, Harry reached over and hung up the phone. The look on Jannings's face puzzled him. There was satisfaction there. And a challenge. But there was also something else. Something hard to pin down.

Harry stood up and took the computer sheet from his jacket. He unfolded it and laid it on the desk in front of Jannings.

"Ballistics. It'll check out."

Harry turned and walked out of the office. He could feel the heat of Jannings's glare on his back. The chief was seething, ready to blow. Harry left the station before he did. Once in his car, Harry checked the sheets of paper that Bennett had slipped him. He popped opened his glove box and withdrew a San Paulo street map. He'd bought it the night before at one of the bookshops on Oceana Mall. He'd had a hunch it might prove useful in the days to come.

He looked up a road in the index and traced the position of the section he wanted. He calculated the best route there, returned the map to the glove box and the papers to his pocket, and started his car.

Twenty minutes later and some eight miles northeast of San Paulo, Harry drove off of Bell Canyon Road and onto a short, hooking dirt trail called Manning Road. At the end of it, Harry came to a squat, one-story ramshackle house. At one time it may have been painted and its roof may have been level and the ground around it may have been clear and clean, but now it was faded and warped, falling in on itself and surrounded by assorted junk and debris.

It was the residence of one Ramona Parkins.

Harry left his car and weaved through the refuse to the front door. He knocked but got no response. He knocked and hollered for Ray but still got no answer. He took a small leather kit from his back pocket and extracted from it a short metal tool.

He inserted this into the keyhole under the loose doorknob and in less than five seconds was standing in the kitchen of the house.

Its interior was no more attractive than its exterior. The furnishings must have been rejected by Goodwill and the decor must have been created by a blind manic-depressive.

Harry's nose prickled at the cloud of musty dust that filled the little house and at the pungent odor that lurked beneath the other smell. The telltale sign of bad plumbing.

In spite of the aroma, Harry started to check out the place.

At that moment Ray Parkins was staring at the line of customers in front of her register. If one more dumb bitch left the line in the middle of her ring-up to go fetch something she'd forgotten, Ray was going to scream and then punch the dildo's lights out. They never came right back. They always had to get one more thing and then everybody else in line started pissin' and moanin'. It was a lousy pain in the ass. And the little old ladies with the goddamned coupons that were for another store or for another brand or had run out two months before. It was a zoo and the lousy day wasn't half done. Ray wasn't feeling too well. A hangover was making her scalp feel shrunk fit to her skull but a couple of sizes too small. She was tired and, though she hated to admit it, nervous. Besides checking groceries and detergents and produce, she was checking the face of every woman customer that passed through or near her station. Wilburn and Kruger were assholes but they weren't defenseless children. They could both take care of themselves and had done so more than a few times. Yet the bitch had gotten both of them. She must be good. Maybe some people do change.

Ray chuckled to herself and counted out a man's change. She moved to bag his stuff and was just deciding to hit Ginley's Bar on her lunch break for a little hair of the dog that bit her when she felt someone tap her shoulder.

She whirled around, expecting to read some dumb cluck the riot act about waiting her turn, and saw a shortish, muscular young man with long black hair and a pencil-thin mustache.

She forgot her customers, her hangover, and her anxieties when she saw him. She hurried around her checkout stand and threw her arms around her visitor. "*Mick*. What the hell you doin' here?" Her smile was bright and wide.

He shrugged himself out of her embrace and stepped backward. 'I hear we got ourselves a problem?"

"How'd you know? I been tryin' to call you. But none of the numbers work anymore."

"Yeah, well, I move around a lot."

"How the hell'd you find out?"

"There are ways."

"Sure. Who the hell cares? The important thing is that you're here." She raised her arms in a clumsy half attempt at embracing him again. He sidestepped his distance from her and looked over at her line of customers, who were growing increasingly impatient.

"Let's get out of here, Ray. We got to go somewhere we can talk."

"Sure, Mick, sure. Anything you say." She lowered her voice. "I'll say I got the curse and can't cope. That'll get me out of here. But I don't, you know."

"So?"

"Well, I just . . . wanted you to . . . You go wait for me outside. I'll be there in a couple of minutes."

Mike walked away before she could try another hug. With wide eyes and a toothy grin she watched him go.

Harry checked the bathroom, the parlor, and the bedroom. The dust and the smell got no better. He found no one. He became aware that, aside from soiled laundry, dirty dishes, empty beer cans, countless cigarette butts, and the moldy remains of half-eaten meals, there were no objects in the house that recorded or indicated the personal history of its occupant. There was nothing at all in any of the rooms to give witness that the inhabitant did anything more here than fulfill the basic requirements of human biology. There were no signs of life, only of existence.

He thought of his own apartment in San Francisco. Well, shit, his was a whole lot cleaner. And he did have a picture. He looked at it sometimes, too. A picture of his wife. Long dead but never forgotten. The victim of a vehicular man-slaughter. The perpetrator being under the influence. That was legal-speak for a drunk who lost control and blew her off the street one night. One senseless night. A long time ago. He had been working. A tough case. He broke it. But when he went home, there was no one there. She never did come home. He'd put in a lot of extra hours since then. Half the time without pay. But, then, who the hell becomes a cop for the money? It's the respect and the gratitude. And, of course, helping justice to be done is its own reward.

Yeah, sure. What the hell sent him off on that bender?

He remembered and returned to the bedroom. He began to search the drawers of a shabby old dresser and found something in the third one.

It was a yellowed, dog-eared, slightly out-of-focus Instamatic snapshot of two young people, a girl and a boy. The girl was red-haired and freckled. The boy was dark-haired and muscular. She was grinning and had an arm looped around his neck. He was scowling and had his arms folded in front of him.

Ray. She was a little brassy and more than a little bovine even then. The boy. He had the poison look of a mean one.

Harry recognized him from the graduation photo of Jannings's son.

Yeah, maybe things were laying out.

He tucked the picture back under the small pile of clean panties in the drawer and left the house.

Back in San Paulo, he consulted Bennett's sheets once more and drove to the E-Z Stop Market. A balding, harried manager type told him that Ray had gotten sick with "female troubles" and taken the remainder of the day off.

Harry thanked him and drove to Ginley's Bar. Once his eyes had adjusted to the murky interior, he looked around the place. Ray was not there. He looked over and spotted the bartender from a couple of nights before. One of the many people so broken up by the news of the death of their pal Wilburn.

Harry approached him. "You work the day and night shift, huh? A real overachiever, aren't you, pal?"

The bartender had been lounging back against the draft-beer dispenser. He straightened up now. "What's it to you, buddy?"

"Ray Parkins been in today?"

"Why the hell should I tell you?"

"Because I'm asking you real nice. You want me to put the question a little differently?"

The bartender squeezed his hands into fists as he thought it over. He looked into Harry's eyes and made his decision. "No, she hasn't, not yet." He unclenched his fists.

"She keep any regular hours?"

"Ray? Shit, no. Whenever she's got money or thinks she can get it, she's here. She's always got the thirst."

"Know any of her friends?"

"Nope."

"You don't huh? What about Kruger? He was here the other night."

"The guy that got shot? Christ, that was awful. Makes my damn bowels crawl just thinkin' about it."

"Did you know him?"

"Look, buddy, I ain't been working here but a couple months. And the people drink here . . . you respect their privacy. Get what I mean?"

Harry nodded and walked toward the exit.

13

Mick and Ray sat at her kitchen table. Mick leaned back on two legs of an old, squeaky wooden kitchen chair and put his feet up on the chipped table. He wore old waterstained boots, faded black corduroys, a ragged striped shirt, and a frayed denim jacket. Ray wore a man's long-sleeved undershirt which she had pulled out of her jeans, and brown scuffy work boots.

They were finishing the first of the several six-packs they'd picked up on the way out to the house. Empties littered the table in front of them, as did open packages of potato chips, pretzels, slim jims, beer nuts, and Twinkies.

"What do we do?" Ray asked, wiping beer foam from her lips. She was seated close to Mick at the table.

"We snuff her," he said, biting into a Twinkie.

"How? This town's got thousands of people. Maybe she ain't even stayin' here." She reached over to wipe white cake cream from Mick's chin. He flinched slightly but allowed her to do it. She took obvious pleasure in the activity. "How do we find her?"

"We don't," Mick answered, and washed down a mouthful of Twinkie with a mouthful of beer.

"What do you mean?"

"We wait. She's got to come for you sometime, right?" Ray nodded. "And she don't think I'm in town, right?" Ray nodded again. "Well, then, it's simple." He reached inside his belt, under his jacket, and yanked out a nine-millimeter automatic. "We'll be here," he said, fingering the gun barrel in a slow, smooth caress. "We'll make her feel real welcome."

Ray looked at the gun and Mick's fondling fingers. She pulled out her own weapon and laid it on the table. "Yeah, real welcome," she said gleefully. She popped open two more beers and handed one to Mick, who took a long pull on it. Ray took a much smaller sip and asked, "What about Alby?"

Mick slammed his can on the table. The force of the hit spewed foamy beer through the hole in its top. "I don't give a fuck about Tyrone," he yelled.

"Okay, Mick, okay." Ray tried to soothe him. "Take it easy. What about Alby?"

Mick calmed himself. "Alby's covered."

"Oh, Mick, come on," she said. "How's Alby covered? He's a zombie. He can't even tell if he's pissin' himself."

Mick slapped his hand flat and hard on the table. The snacks and beer cans jumped. One empty rolled off and bounced along the floor. "Alby's covered," he shouted.

Ray threw up her hands in front of her. "Okay, Mickey, boy. Okay." She shrugged and picked up her gun. Smiling, she began to finger its barrel. "We'll wait, baby, just like you say. We'll make her feel real welcome."

Mick watched her and smiled at the thought.

• • •

The clerk behind the counter was young and sandy-haired. He had just told Harry that Tyrone had not come to work.

"Do you know where he is?"

"No," the clerk answered. Harry looked at the kid's name tab; scott was hand printed on it in block letters.

"Do you know where he might be?"

"No, I don't. It's unusual for Mr. Tyrone to be absent without making previous arrangements."

"Did he call in today?"

"No, he didn't. That's kind of unusual, too. He always calls even if he's going to be just a little late."

"Did anyone here at the store call him?"

"Yes, I did, myself."

"Well?"

"Well what?"

This clerk is real quick, thought Harry. A real up-and-comer. Or maybe he's just experienced in the "you ask me a question and I answer it but tell you nothing" routine.

"What did Tyrone say?"

"Nothing. There was no answer at his house."

No answer. Harry knew what his next stop would be. He exited the hardware store and went to his car. He found Tyrone's house with no problem and parked in front of it.

Harry looked around at the half-settled development. He noted that Tyrone's nearest neighbor was a good hundred yards away. With the right conditions, properly nurtured, murder could do very well here. Harry got out of his car and went to Tyrone's front door. No one answered the bell or his knocking. He tried the door but it was locked. Judging from the quality of the home's construction and the pleasing, artful layout of the housing tract, Harry was sure that the lock on the door would be of the finest craftsmanship, a secure, burglarproof, tamperproof piece of work. He took out his small kit

Three seconds later, he was standing inside Tyrone's house.

The place was sparsely furnished. Either the contractor was late getting the house into shape or Tyrone couldn't wait to move into his beige-and-brown badge of prosperity. The parlor and dining-room area were empty except for unpacked cardboard cartons and large shopping bags of appliances and household etceteras. The bags were all stenciled with Tyrone's store logo. Harry had no doubt as to where their contents had been obtained.

The kitchen was also empty except for a card table and two metal folding chairs. The remains of a coffee-and-doughnuts breakfast for one were spread out and moldering on the table.

Harry was leaving the kitchen, intending to search the second floor, when he saw light glowing in the space beneath a closed door next to the brand-new dishwasher.

He opened the door and looked around the garage. Everything seemed to be in order. The Buick was parked nicely, not too close to the wall. The drive space was clear of obstacles. The sides and corners were stacked high with the requisite boxes and tools. The garage was just like any other. Except for the corpse. It was lying on its back, hands clasped to a bloody crotch, head perforated by a small, round darkly clotted hole.

Harry studied the face below the red dot and recalled Janning's kid's graduation photo. As well as he could figure, this face matched a younger version of itself in the photograph.

Wilburn, Kruger, and now Tyrone.

Three out of six and still counting.

A connection was getting awfully goddamned obvious.

A question needed to be asked.

Harry found Tyrone's phone and called the San Paulo

station to report the killing. As he waited for somebody to show, he thought about that question. He knew who should be asked. And he thought he knew what the response would be. He decided to try Ray Parkins once more instead. A confrontation with Jannings was unavoidable and he knew it would be messy. He'd best go in with the strongest hand possible.

After a short while Harry heard the sirens. They came close. He went outside to meet them. Police cars, an ambulance, reporters, and spectators converged on the house. He watched the police chief's car pull up. Jannings got out. The corners of his mouth and eyes drooped lower than ever. His hair was mussed as though he'd run his hands roughly over his head. His tie, though pulled tight to his neck, was half turned under a wing of his collar. His head was bowed, his shoulders stooped. He looked very tired.

Harry pointed the first arrivals toward the garage and moved on to intercept the chief.

Jannings looked up to see him approaching but did not stop walking.

"You don't give up, do you, Callahan?" he said as he stepped past Harry on his way to the crime scene.

"It's my job," Harry called to him. "Remember?"

Jannings stopped and turned slowly to face Harry. "What do you want from me?" There was more fatigue and stress in his voice than anger.

"I want to know why you're dragging your ass on this investigation."

Jannings stepped close to Harry. "I'm doing all I can. Every available man is on the street. Patrols have been tripled. Leaves and days off are canceled. This department's logging more overtime than the township can afford to pay. We'll get this maniac."

Maniac? Harry examined Jannings's face and eyes. The

fatigue, the exasperation, the stress, wove a heavy curtain. For the moment it was impenetrable.

"You can't believe these killings are random?"

Jannings raised his voice slightly. "I reject no theory at this time. I am following all possible leads. And in case you haven't noticed, there's been no truce declared on muggings or shoplifting or burglaries or drunk driving or any of the other less headline-grabbing crimes we face every day. The less interesting crimes that hot-shit homicide detectives thumb their noses at. Look around, big shot, we're doing the best we can."

The curtain was beginning to tear. Anger was flashing, hot and ravenous. Was there something else there, too?

"It's not good enough," Harry said, taking time to drive each word home.

Jannings's neck began to redden above his collar. "Callahan, for the last—repeat—last time. This is not your jurisdiction." The color rose past his jaw, up to his shaggy eyebrows. "This is not your case. Stay out of it." His forehead was flushed, too. "I'm warning you."

He turned abruptly and started to walk away.

Harry called to him. "Hey, Jannings."

The police chief turned around. There was something else in his eyes. Harry was sure of it now.

"Don't you want to ask me why I was here?"

Jannings threw back his head and stretched his mouth wide. He roared at the sky. Harry could see the tendons cording out in his neck. Flecks of spit collected at the edges of his mouth. The deep, guttural growling stopped as suddenly as it had begun. The police chief lowered his head, balled his fists, and charged Harry.

Harry had no trouble sidestepping Jannings's run. The chief then spun around and swung wildly at his head. Harry avoided the swipe easily and readied himself to dodge another assault but it never came. Two police officers had rushed over and were struggling to restrain their furious superior. Jannings was raving now. 'You son of a bitch, Callahan. You goddamned bastard.''

Harry turned away from the stumbling, tugging trio and walked to his car.

He knew what lurked behind the anger and the fatigue and the stress.

Fear.

The sun was down and the sky was blue-black when Jenny turned onto Manning Road. She followed it around and came to the dilapidated house. The woods were dense and the darkness around the house was complete. She stopped her car several yards down the road from the clearing in front of the place. She sat for a moment and watched. Light shone through the window to the right of the front door. It was the only light in the house.

So this was where Ray lived, she thought. How appropriate. How disgustingly fitting. Some people don't change, do they?

Jenny had never seen this house before. She wondered if it was the house of Ray's youth. Had she lived here as a young girl? With parents? Had she slept here at night, dreaming a young girl's dreams, feeling a young girl's melancholy and elation? Had she lain awake at night, disturbed by a young girl's fears, excited by a young girl's hopes? Had she sneaked off to the bathroom in the quiet of early morning to stare at herself in the mirror and, behind a locked door, to chart the progress of change in a young girl's body? Had she wondered what sprouting hair and rounding buttocks and swelling breasts really meant? Had she run her hands over those metamorphosing areas and felt pride in the change and confidence in the notion that she, and she alone, would be the keeper, the guardian, the dispenser of private places and private thoughts and private feelings?

Jenny also wondered if Ray had ever stood in the bathroom of this house, again behind a locked door, again staring at herself in the mirror, but this time charting cuts and bruises and bite marks. She wondered if Ray had ever stood beneath a scalding, cutting shower stream, frantically rubbing herself, desperate to scrub her body clean of sand and blood and shame.

Jenny could hear the ocean, though she knew it was nowhere near her. She would always be able to hear the ocean. Always be able to wrap herself in the inevitability of its tide, the peace of its depth, the security of its infinite waving.

The ocean had saved her that night.

It had not deserted her. It had stayed by her side throughout. It had been there afterward. Whispering the last consolation she heard. Giving the last tranquillity she felt. The ocean would be with her always.

She saw the light in the house go out. There was total darkness for a moment. Then a smaller, less powerful light went on. The window to the left of the front door lit up.

Jenny reached into her bag and withdrew her gloves and her weapon. She put on the gloves and checked the cylinder. Six cartridges correctly in place. She slid the .38 back into her bag and looped her arm through its strap. She was ready. Time to go.

She opened the door carefully and got out of the car. She closed it noiselessly and slowly approached the house, clinging to the cover of the line of trees bordering the road. She thought at first that the night was silent and still, but as she

neared the squalid little house she became aware of the
myriad insect sounds, the rustling of leaves, the creaking of
branches. The grass between the trees was thick and high but
she could see motion there. Bugs flying and crawling, small
animals scurrying. She came to the end of the treeline. She
would have to cross a short section of open ground here. The
light from the window was weaker than the light that had
preceded it but was still sufficient to expose. For a brief
instant she would be vulnerable. She had to assume that Ray
would be vigilant. After Kruger she would have guessed. She
might even be waiting now. Luring, gloating.

Jenny remembered the day it had all started. An ordinary,
uneventful day, like so many others that had come before it
during her time at the University of California at San Paulo.
She had been an art-history major. She wanted, even then, to
paint but she planned to support herself by teaching. She had
been the model student. Better-than-average grades, active in
extracurriculars, and, because of a part-time job at a plant
nursery in town, self-sufficient. The world was a bright,
friendly place for her then. Each day was filled with promise
and joy and discovery.

Of course there were problems. Small ones. But they were
to be overcome. They were to be learned from. There was
another girl working at the nursery. A town girl. Jenny
immediately sensed her animosity and resentment when she
met her. She was a rough sort. Crude and sometimes nasty.
But sometimes funny, too. Distant and brooding. But sometimes friendly and talkative, too. Jenny had never known
which personality the girl would assume each day. Sometimes
she changed back and forth on the same day. Jenny tried her
best to understand the girl. She thought perhaps she could be
a friend to her. Maybe that's what she needed. Just like

anybody else. A friend. Somebody to talk to. Somebody to understand.

One day—a particularly sunny and breezy day, as Jenny recalled—this girl had approached her. She was smiling, laughing, making jokes about the couple who owned the nursery. Then she asked Jenny a question. A simple, rather meaningless little question. Or so Jenny had thought.

She remembered it well. Every word. Every gesture. Every nuance. How could she have been so stupid? It was all there, plain to see and hear. Plain to understand. Why hadn't she understood?

"You comin' to that party I told you about?" the girl had asked her that day. "Listen, I'll drive. You don't have to worry about gettin' back."

"No, Ray, I can't. Really," Jenny told her that same day. "My sister's coming up to visit me for the weekend."

"Oh, yeah, how about that? Ain't that something? Tell me, is sissy a college girl, too, like you?"

"Oh, no. Not yet, at least. She's just a junior in high school."

"Well, listen, honey, don't worry about it. Bring her along with you. The more, the merrier."

"No, Ray, I really don't think so."

"Hey, what's the big deal? Is it because we're townies? Huh, is that it? Is that what's the matter, us locals not good enough for you?"

"No, Ray. That's not it at all. You misunderstand me. I didn't mean anything like that."

"Then come along."

"Well . . . you're driving?"

"Sure."

"And you'll take us back to my dorm?"

"Yeah, I said I would, didn't I?"

"And you'll take us when we want to go?"

"*Jesus*. What is this? You comin' or not?"

"Allright, we'll come. But we have to leave early. I want to be sure you understand."

"I understand fine. You two missie's can leave whenever you want to. But who knows? You may have yourselves a good time."

Jenny thought about that brief, meaningless conversation. She had been very stupid. The intonations, the facial expressions, the truths. Why hadn't she recognized them? Why hadn't she known?

If not for her own sake, then for Elizabeth's.

It was too late now. Now she could only do what she could do. To make up. Not to make right. To pay back. Not enough. Revenge. Not justice.

But something.

Gripping her shoulder bag tight to her side, she left the dusky shelter of the trees and crossed the open ground. She hurried into the shadow of the housefront and pressed herself close to its splintery wall.

She listened. There was no sound, no movement.

She edged over to the door. She stepped gingerly onto one of the two steps leading up to it. There was no sound from the wood as it supported her weight. She stepped up to the next level. Still no sound. She reached for the doorknob and heard a car crunching Manning Road's coarse dirt. She turned to see headlights approaching.

She jumped off the step and, hugging the rough wood of the house, rushed around its far corner and threw herself flat against its side wall. The woods came right up to the house on that side and Jenny felt the prodding of branches through her jacket and pants. She pushed herself as close as she could to the house and waited.

Mick was slumped on the couch. The beer had made him drowsy, so he decided to sleep while Ray watched for Jenny. But Ray had moved to the parlor and sat across from him now. She was watching him sleep. She was watching his lips flare slightly as he breathed. The inhaled air played along his nostrils and throat and almost became a snore. She watched his stomach rise with each intake of air.

Ray got up from her battered parlor chair and dropped her gun onto the seat cushion behind her. She crossed the room softly and stood by the couch. She watched Mick breathe. She watched his body flex and contract with every breath. She bent over and delicately slid his automatic out of his waistband. She laid it quietly on a scarred coffee table beside the couch and lifted a leg over his slumbering body. She wedged her knee into the small space between Mick's side and the back of the couch. Then she carefully transferred her weight to her wedged leg and insinuated her body into that same space. Once there, she paused. When she was sure that Mick had not been disturbed, she uncoiled herself and stretched out beside the sleeping man. She smiled and lightly brushed a lock of hair from his wide forehead. She watched his face as he slept, and snuggled closer.

Harry noticed the gray Oldsmobile Firenza and got out of his car to inspect it. He found nothing. Returning to his own car, he radioed the station, asking for Bennett. It took a few minutes for Bennett to come on.

"Bennett here, Inspector. What can I do for you?"

"I want you to run a plate for me, California license one-Adam-Queen-one-seven-five. Got it?"

"Yes, Inspector. But what—"

"Talk to you later." Harry hung up his microphone and drove down to the house.

There was a light on in the parlor area. Somebody was home. Maybe he'd get a chance to ask some questions. Maybe he'd even get some answers.

He left his car.

Jenny heard the car come close and stop. She heard its door open and close. She heard footsteps. Someone was walking toward the house. She held her breath and thought about trying to back up into the woods. She leaned back a fraction of an inch and felt the light scratch of leaves against her neck and cheek. She also heard the rustle of branches. She stopped moving immediately and pressed forward against the house again.

Ray gently caressed Mick's forehead. She began to unbutton the few buttons remaining on his shirt. She brushed her lips over the hairless skin of his chest. She moved herself close against his side and raised a leg softly onto his legs. She began to caress his shoulder and arm and leg as she started to rub herself against him.

She was starting to unbuckle his belt when Mick woke up. His eyes bulged their drowsiness away when he saw her face hovering over his. His lips pulled back over his teeth when he felt her up against him.

"What the fuck are you *doin'*?" he screamed at her, then looked down to see her hand on his belt.

Ray froze, surprised and suddenly afraid.

Mick grabbed her shirt and pulled hard while twisting his body away from her. She flew over him and off the couch, smashing her back and head against the ratty coffee table.

"Mick, wait a minute," she yelled. "You don't get it. I was only trying' . . ."

She struggled to her feet as Mick jumped off the couch. When she was standing, he whacked her across the face with an open hand. Her head snapped to the side. Before she could speak or cry out, he viciously backhanded her and knocked her off her feet. She yelped with pain as her rib cage slammed into the side of the coffee table.

"You fuckin' *pig*! Don't you ever put your hands on me, you understand?" He howled at her as he lifted her off the floor and hurled her against the parlor wall.

Ray coughed as the air was pressed out of her lungs when she hit the wall. She tried to explain but the words would not form. She felt blood oozing from her nose onto her lips and crumpled to the floor.

Mick leaped the distance between them and kicked her in the thigh. Ray whined with pain. As she grabbed at her leg he kicked her in the stomach

She started to gag but still wound herself tightly in a ball to protect herself from the beating she knew was coming.

Mick was standing over her now. "You fuckin' *pig*. I'll . . . I'll . . ." His rage cut off his powers of speech. It rendered him mute with fury. He kicked again and again.

Suddenly the front door crashed in.

Harry heard the screaming as he approached the house. He'd heard this kind of thing before. Not too many times and never with this raw intensity. But there was no mistaking it. Somebody was getting beaten to death.

He drew his Magnum and, with his shoulder leading, threw himself at the flimsy front door. It shattered under his attack and Harry burst into the house. With three giant steps he leaped into the parlor and saw Ray Parkins curled up in a corner of the room, on the floor, getting her life kicked out of her.

Harry extended his gun arm and was about to yell to the short, well-built young man standing over Ray to stop when the man spun around and with lightning speed kicked the Magnum out of his hand and across the room.

Before Harry could react to the swipe, the guy twisted back around, jumped straight up in the air, and lashed out with his other foot. The full force of the kick caught Harry at his solar plexus. His breath shot out of his lungs as a fireball of pain exploded in his chest. He crashed backward against the doorjamb and the guy was instantly on him. He felt his knees kicked out from under him. He hit the floor and felt the guy press his advantage with a flurry of follow-up kicks. Harry knew immediately that he must get up off the floor or he would be no match for the kicker. He also knew from the sheer rage that was being unleashed upon him that this guy, whoever he was, would not stop until one Harry Callahan, inspector, San Francisco PD, was dead meat.

Harry rolled away from the barrage of kicks and won a few seconds' letup. But it was short lived. The guy followed him and doubled his frenzied attack. Harry took shots in the stomach, the chest, and the back. Each one was a hammer. His ribs wouldn't take much more and his head and throat wouldn't take one.

He rolled again but this time right at the guy, bumping into his stationary leg as his other leg was extended behind him, preparing for another kick. Harry wasn't able to knock the guy off his feet but he forced him to stumble over him and so gained a few crucial seconds. As the guy regained his balance Harry came up onto his knees. When the wild man resumed his bombardment, Harry was able to counter the kicks with his forearms. He also calculated their rhythm.

The guy was mid-kick when Harry jumped up and to the side in a crouching position. It was too late for his attacker to react, so he could do nothing but follow through with the kick. Harry grabbed his ankle and twisted roughly while at the same time springing up from his crouch. He lifted the guy off his other leg and heaved him into the air. The guy flipped heels over head and came crashing down on the coffee table, smashing it to bits. He came up fast, more shocked than hurt.

Harry was on him in a second.

A series of jabs stung him and kept him from attacking. The final jab set him up nicely and a right followed it to smash his nose. A left snapped his head sideways and a combination doubled him over. But before Harry could put him down, he was attacked from behind. Somebody had jumped on his back and was pounding his head.

He shook himself violently and knocked his new assailant to the floor. He turned and saw that it was a bloodied, battered Ray. She started to shout at him.

"Don't you *touch* him, you lousy *shit*."

Harry could not believe it. The punk had nearly kicked her guts out and she was protecting him.

Harry turned back to finish the slime and Ray attacked him again. He had no time to explain things to her, and he could not afford to wrestle with her and so give her pal time to recover. The scum was definitely mental and definitely lethal. He pushed her away to arm's length and decked her with a short, firm left. She sprawled to the floor and smacked up against the wall.

In the meantime, her friend was straightening up and shaking his head in an attempt to clear the brain. Harry moved in and slammed a right into the guy's gut. As his head dipped, Harry threw a left to the side of his head.

The guy went down and stayed down.

Harry caught his breath and searched for his Magnum. As he found and holstered it he saw Ray crawl across the debris of the coffee table to comfort the man who would have killed her. She knelt by him and lifted his head onto her lap. She wiped away the blood from his eyes and mouth.

"Mick? You hurt, baby? Mickey?" She looked up at Harry, hate blazing in her eyes. "You *hurt* him," she screamed. "You fuckin' bastard. I'll *kill* you for this." She went back to caring for her man. "Mick . . . Mickey, baby—"

Harry crossed to them and yanked Ray away from the fallen man. "I'm a police officer," he told her. "And I got questions for you. You better have answers.

"I ain't got a fuckin' word for you, you son of a bitch. I got a right to a lawyer."

The punk was coughing and gagging himself back into consciousness. Harry grabbed a handful of hair and dragged him to his feet.

"You're coming with me, asshole."

The guy's tongue was drooping out of his mouth: his eyes were crossed but he was still defiant.

"You suck my ass with straws," he gurgled at Harry.

Harry shoved him forward, bouncing him off the wall, then caught him and pulled him out of the room.

"I'll be back," he told Ray, and left the house.

"Where you takin' him, you bastard?" She ran through the doorway and watched Harry drag Mick to his car. "I'll get a lawyer, you fuckin' shit. He'll be out tomorrow, bastard. We'll fuckin' sue you, you son of a bitch."

Harry started the car and drove off.

Ray watched them disappear into the blackness of the night, then turned and walked back into the kitchen. She swayed as she made her dazed way over to the refrigerator and leaned on it for support. She wiped the blood from her

nose and lips on the sleeve of her shirt. She stood still for a
moment and gasped air into her lungs. When she had regained
her normal breathing rhythm, she opened the refrigerator and
yanked out a beer. Still unsteady on her feet, she pushed the
door closed and leaned back on the refrigerator as she popped
the top of the can. Beer foamed up through the hole and over
her fingers to drip to the floor. She ignored this, lifted the can
to her lips, and took a long swallow. Foam spilled out of her
mouth and dripped down her chin onto her chest. The cold
liquid tingled as it ran down between her breasts. She giggled
at its tickle.

Trusting her walk, she pushed away from the refrigerator and
unsteadily traipsed into the parlor. She dropped onto the couch
and stretched herself. Her thighs, ribs, and back were beginning to ache. She knew she'd have some purple welts in the
morning. She'd probably have to call in sick and miss another
day's work. And pay. But what the hell, she had things to do
tomorrow anyway. She had to call some shyster lawyer and
spring Mick. That was the most important thing. She set her
beer down on the floor and unlaced her work boots. When she
had pulled them and her socks off, she retrieved her drink and
lifted it to her mouth. She took a long pull on the beer as she
leaned back on the couch and wiggled her toes.

As she lowered the can she saw someone standing in the
shadows of the kitchen. For a brief, fleeting instant she
thought that it was Mick, returning to her after somehow
overpowering the bastard cop. But then the someone stepped
through the doorway and into the dimly lit parlor.

It was her.

Ray smiled. "So, the bitch is here."

Jenny had drawn her gun from her shoulder bag before
stepping around the bashed front door. She held it now, her

arm at her side, her fingers gently squeezing its grip. She peered through the room's murky, yellow light and stared at the grinning creature slouched on the couch in front of her. This less-than-human aberration had proved to be one of the central characters in the tragedy of Jenny's life. One of the pivotal actors in the barren, desperate story of Elizabeth's wasted existence.

This slatternly woman who had hardly known her and who had never seen Elizabeth. Not once, Not one single time had she laid eyes on that bright, lovely girl of happy spirit and deep affection. That girl that was no more. That teenager who was then so full of life and who had now become a hardened, blocked-out, hollow shell.

This thing before her had been, if not the instigator of the horror, then certainly its Judas goat.

The knowledge of all this nearly overwhelmed her. She began to tremble. She wanted to speak but could not. Her voice might betray her resolve. She must not risk her purpose.

But she did want very much to speak. She wanted to ask a single question that had become one of the chief ghosts that haunted her sleeping nights and dreaming days.

Jenny wanted to ask why.

Why had she done it?

Jenny stared at Ray's face. The grin had become wider. The eyes had become slits of mockery. It was as though she had read Jenny's thoughts and now ridiculed her for having them.

Ray's grin became a laugh as she threw back her head and cackled in high-pitched derision.

Jenny remembered the taunting, debasing noise very well. It had provided a staccato background to the hours of torture and defilement. The ravaging and violation that went on and on and promised to never end. The cruel, brute faces that leared down at her. The sweating foreheads. The matted hair. The slack jaws. The shoving. The joking. The bragging. And the insults. The venomous degradation of the name-calling and cursing. And the violence. Beyond the sheer savagery of the probing and mounting and thrusting, there were so many punches and slaps and pinches. Hands pressed so hard on her wrists and ankles and mouth. She had tried to scream through the clamping palms but no sound passed them. She had tried to bite them away but had only been struck by other hands. She had twisted her head so she could see her sister. No hands held her but Elizabeth did not move. She did not blink. Her eyes were blank. No hands blocked her mouth but she did not scream.

Jenny remembered the tears had come to her then. They had welled-up and flowed out of her eyes.

The beasts that were devouring her had paused, readying themselves for their next assault.

She had tried hard to listen to the sea, but the cackling noise had interfered. Then it had stopped and become speech. Gloating, triumphant, evil.

"*Split* the bitch. How's it feel, goody-two-shoes college cunt?"

The cackle came back.

It was in front of her now.

Ray stopped laughing and glanced quickly around the debris-strewn floor. Her own weapon was out of reach, on the chair by the far wall. But Mick's nine-millimeter was around somewhere.

She spotted it and gauged the distance between it and her. It was more than a few feet. But a single, quick move might do it. Now, while the bitch was spacing out.

Jenny's eyes came back into focus as she pushed the dream out of her mind. She stared at Ray. There was something different about her. Her eyes were changed. They were calculating, scheming.

Ray noticed the change in Jenny and sneered at her. "Tell me . . . how's your slut sister?'

The words stabbed Jenny's heart like a jagged dagger.

Ray hurled the beer can at her and jumped off the couch toward the gun.

Jenny ducked. Beer sprayed her face as the can flew by her head. Her two arms sprang up in front of her and she fired.

The bullet took Ray at her forehead, just above her left eye. Skin, bits of bone, and a splash of blood flew out of a small round hole as the slug entered her skull. It exited the rear of her head and spattered her brains across the faded, threadbare couch.

Ray began to twitch her life away.

Jenny stepped close and stood over her, arms outstretched, and fired again. Ray's body stopped squirming.

Jenny exhaled a long, slow breath and relaxed the tension in her legs and arms and groin. She turned to leave and was startled to find someone looking at her. She threw her arms up in front of her and aimed her gun.

Then she realized she was looking into a mirror.

She was looking at herself. She studied herself. The spread, half-bent legs. The extended arms. The steady hands. The round dark hole of the gun barrel. Her face above and behind it.

And most of all, her eyes.

She fired.

The mirror shattered into many pieces.

Jenny ran from the house with the sounds of the tinkling, jangling shards of glass ringing in her ears.

14

Harry drove straight to the San Paulo police station after cuffing his prisoner and reading him his rights. The punk dummied up completely. He wouldn't give his name. He wouldn't even curse at Harry.

Harry thought he recognized the face. Years of violence and dissipation had taken their toll, but Harry thought he looked an awful lot like the one remaining boy in the graduation photo.

When they arrived at the station, Harry pulled the sleaze out of the car and pushed him, headfirst, through the swinging double doors of the squad room. He shoved him to the long counter and told the surprised desk sergeant to book the punk for resisting arrest, assaulting an officer, and possession of an unconcealed, dangerously ugly face.

He looked over at Janning's office. It was empty

Jenny drove home and nearly tore the clothes from her body as she stripped and rushed into the bathroom. She let the shower run until its needle streams of water were streaming. Then she stepped under the spray and let it sluice over her. It pounded her skin and flushed it red. It beat on her head and massaged her scalp to a tingle. When her whole body had been worked over by the steaming, streaming water, she lowered its temperature and soaped herself clean. Then she shampooed her hair. After rinsing off, she lowered the hot water until the cold snatched her breath away and stood shivering under it until she could take it no longer.

She left the shower and, after toweling off, put on her robe and went to her living-room picture window. She looked out at the sea but soon turned away from it and crossed to her self-portrait.

She drew away the cover that hid the painting from casual or uninvited view and marked her progress.

It was considerable. A face was nearly complete. Color almost filled the canvas. Jenny looked at herself. Or at least at the image of herself that her mind's eye beheld. She remembered the quotation about the eye seeing "not itself but by reflection."

Jenny stared at the canvas.

So this was herself.

She turned to the mirror she had set up beside the painting. She saw herself there also.

So this was herself, too.

She compared the two images. The faces. The eyes.

Without looking away from the mirror, she reached to her workbench–bureau and felt around its top surface until her hand came to a metal ruler.

She compared the two Jennys one last time, then swung the ruler down on the mirror.

The glass shattered and fell to the floor.

·   ·   ·

Mick stood at the pay phone in the corridor in front of the lockup area. After his allotted one phone call the police officer standing a few feet to his side would lead him to a holding cell.

Mick inserted a dime in the coin slot and angled his body so that the officer could not see what number he dialed.

He listened for the connection to be made and then waited for the ringing to begin.

The connection went through. The ringing began.

No one answered at the other end.

Mick waited as it rang some more.

Still there was no answer.

Mick let it go on ringing.

The policeman began to grow fidgety. He looked at his watch and decided to wait one minute more.

Mick listened to the ringing.

The officer moved over to him and tapped him on the elbow. "Time enough, buddy. Let's go."

Mick pulled his arm away from the cop's touch and slammed the receiver onto its cradle.

The policeman led him to his cell.

Police Chief Jannings exhaled and relaxed. He was at home, sitting in a comfortable, overstuffed parlor chair.

He thanked God that the phone had stopped ringing.

Harry unlocked his hotel room door and trudged inside. Pissface was stretched out on the floor. He tilted his head slightly to confirm it was Harry, then plopped himself back to sleep.

Harry unzipped his jacket and tossed it onto a chair, then he walked to the bed and sat down. The mattress squeaked under him.

He was tired and sore. The punk was pretty good with his feet. He'd let the slime stew overnight and interrogate him in the morning. He wasn't very optimistic about the potential results of that examination because the punk looked as if he knew how to keep his mouth shut.

Ray Parkins was certainly no soft touch but she might scope out as a better lead. He'd let her stew awhile, too, maybe go back later tonight or early tomorrow morning.

The case was laying out now. He felt very close to its conclusion. He resisted the temptation to theorize and tried to clear his mind of the investigation for the time being. He did not believe in theories. They wasted time and energy. He believed in following the facts relentlessly until they led to a single, ultimate conclusion. Theorists could make any incomplete set of facts pan out to anything they wanted. Or to nothing at all. That was not the Harry Callahan way.

He needed some rest now. And a beer. As a matter of fact, he needed a few beers more than he needed the rest. Then he'd decide whether to brace Ray Parkins in the middle of the night.

The bedsprings groaned as he got up and walked to the small refrigerator on the far side of the room. Light spilled out of it into the dark room as he opened its door. It was empty.

Damn it. Now he'd have to go out. He remembered the liquor store on Beach Street a few blocks down from La Bahía.

He put his jacket on and left.

Something finally broke right and easy for him in San Paulo. He made the store just before closing. As he started back along Beach Street to his hotel the lights in the store were extinguished.

He pulled a can free of the plastic rope that bound the

six-pack together amd walked along the bike path above the sandline of the beach. The street was deserted. It was almost eleven o'clock and the night was a little too cool for strollers.

Harry sipped his beer and looked out at the breakers. It was a different ocean here from what it was around San Francisco. Up there it was more forthright. It was commercial or scenic or recreational or calm or choppy or all those things at the same time. But whatever it was, it was always up front and direct. Here it was more subtle, more inscrutable.

As Harry walked along he became aware of a figure standing on the beach, close to the surf. It was a woman. Her blonde hair was ruffling in the wind. Jenny Spenser.

He left the bicycle path and crossed the beach in her direction.

He was almost at her side when she sensed his presence. She was staring out at the almost invisible horizon when she turned quickly to face him. She was surprised but, he felt, not frightened. When she recognized him, she turned back to the darkness of the sea and sky.

"A little late for wave watching," he said.

"I couldn't sleep."

He pulled a can from the plastic rope and offered it to her. "Beer?"

She looked at him, then at the beer. "Thank you," she said, accepting the can. She popped the tab and drank.

Harry sipped his. "It's not safe to be out alone in the dark."

"Life's full of risks, isn't it?" she said softly.

They drank beer and looked out at the ocean.

"I'd better get home," she said. "Thanks again for the beer." She turned to walk away.

"Did you bicycle down?"

"No. I walked. It relaxes me."

"I'll give you a ride home."

"No, thank you, that's allright."

"It's okay," Harry told her. "It relaxes me."

They drove out to West Cliff in silence. That suited Harry just fine. He hated small talk and, consequently, was never any good at it. This woman seemed to go easy on the bullshit, too. He liked that about her. But there was something else that attracted him. Something indefinable and shadowy.

He glanced over at her. She sat by the passenger door with her knees close but not tight together. Her hands lay in her lap, palms up, her fingers half-bent. She looked straight ahead but it seemed to Harry that she watched something that could be seen only by her.

"Here it is." It was the first time she'd spoken since giving him directions.

He slowed down and pulled over to stop in front of a small cliffside house.

"Thank you for the lift." She got out of the car and shut the door. She took a step away but then stopped and stood still a few seconds. Harry stared at her back and was about to get out of the car himself, to see if something had frightened or distracted her, when she turned and walked back to the car. She opened the door and leaned in.

"You feel like something stronger than beer?"

Harry looked at her. Her skin was very white and very smooth and her face was just a little less shadowy. There was an openness—tiny and maybe fleeting but new to her.

"Sure."

"Come in, then."

He followed her to the house.

When she had unlocked the door and led him in, she

switched on a lamp and took off her jacket. "I'll get some brandy," she said, and left the room.

Harry looked around. The easels set up by the picture-window wall caught his attention immediately. A canvas leaned on one of them. The other was empty. The canvas was angled away from him, to catch the light, he supposed, so he could not see if any work had been done on it. Curious to see what sort of stuff she did, he crossed the room to look at it. Must be a terrific place for an artist, he thought as he walked over to the easels. Great light, kind of remote, certainly quiet and peaceful. Nice place to concentrate.

He stepped in front of the canvas and was totally unprepared for what he saw. It was Jenny Spenser's face—he could tell that. Shit, he was a trained observer and investigator—but it had to be another Jenny Spenser. Maybe Jenny Spenser the holocaust victim. Or Jenny Spenser, her soul burning in the eternal flames of hell. Whoever it was, it damn sure wasn't the woman who was now in the kitchen hunting for some decent booze.

Was this what they called artistic license? Harry thought. What the hell . . .

It was like looking into an open wound.

Harry Callahan never bragged that he'd seen it all; but he sure thought he'd seen most of it.

This was something else.

He heard glasses clinking and in a few seconds she reentered the living room.

She stopped short when she saw him in front of her painting. She carried a brandy snifter in each hand and the dark amber liquid sloshed in the glasses as she stood watching him watching her other face.

She recovered quickly from her surprise and her embarrassment, and brought him his drink.

Harry took the brandy and nodded at the painting. "Unusual."

She smiled—a bit awkwardly, he thought—and drew the picture's cover down over it.

As she did this Harry glanced down at the floor beneath the empty easel and saw the shards of mirror glass.

"I have a rule," she said when the cover was in place. "Never drink with a critic."

She looked up at him and smiled again. Easily this time, he noted. Openly. She clinked her glass against his and then drank. He did, too. The brandy warmed his throat and chest as it went down.

She opened her lips slightly and he was sure she was about to speak, but after a second of indecision she sipped from her glass and turned away to gaze out at the dark sea.

Harry could see her face reflected in the glass of the window. She was thinking things, this young, rather odd woman. She always seemed to be thinking things.

Harry was swallowing some more brandy—he still held the glass to his mouth—when she turned back to face him.

Her eyes were wide and less shadowy than he had yet seen them.

"You want to be alone tonight, Callahan?"

Harry lowered his glass and stared at her. She held his gaze and stared right back.

"Neither do I," she said.

15

"You are one royal pain in the ass, buddy," the police officer groaned at Mick.

"Too fuckin' bad, storm trooper. I want my crummy call. Now. You copy, dirt brain?"

The officer slowly shook his head. "You really put it to a test, don't you? It used to be I didn't hold with police brutality. But you're making me a believer and damned fast."

"Go ahead, dork, try touching me. I'll sue your ass so fast you won't know what happened. I already got that son of a bitch who brought me in lined up. What the hell was his name?"

"Callahan. And from what I've heard, you were lucky you could walk in."

"Well, he's gonna need all the luck he can get."

"You threatening an officer of the law?"

"I don't waste my breath on shit like him or you, sucker. Now, gimme my goddamned call."

The officer gritted his teeth and unlocked Mick's cell, then led him to the phone and stood aside as Mick dialed a number and waited.

There was no answer.

Mick hung up and dialed again. Again there was no answer.

He slammed the receiver down and mumbled to himself, "Where the fuck is he?"

The officer moved in to lead him back to his cell, but Mick whirled on him, shouting, "I still got one comin', bastard. I still ain't made it."

The policeman tried to calm him down but Mick was in a frenzy. "I want to make the shittin' call *now*. You gotta let me. It's the law."

The officer hesitated. He wanted badly to wring the rotten punk's neck, but he restrained himself and stepped aside to let him try once more.

Mick calmed down when he saw the cop move aside. He picked his dime out of the return slot and dropped it back into the phone. His mind raced as he waited for the call to go through. He had to call somebody and get back out on the street. Things were getting too confused. He had to put them in order again.

He smiled suddenly. Yeah, he knew who he could call. They still owed him a couple from the good old days. And since it was their sister's husband that got croaked, they should be primed for a little action. Yeah, they'd do nicely. A little too fuckin' slow on the uptake but they tried real hard.

He dialed and, on the third ring, finally got somebody to answer his call.

"Eddie? It's me, Mick. I'm in the slam. Get me the fuck out of here."

•   •   •

Harry sat up in bed. Jenny lay next to him, on her side, facing away. Being careful not to disturb her, he leaned over to see if she was asleep. Her eyes were closed.

He couldn't be sure if he wished she was awake or was glad that she slept. He knew only that he couldn't sleep and that he was leaving.

He looked at her again. Her shoulders were bare. Her skin was smooth and almost as white as the sheet she had pulled up around her. Her blond hair flared out on the pillow beside her head.

Careful, Callahan, he warned himself. Be careful. Doing the job and staying alive are complicated enough.

He pulled back the sheet that covered him and slid out of bed. He dressed quickly, shouldered his holster and Magnum, and left the bedroom.

As he did, Jenny opened her eyes.

She heard the front door quietly close.

Mick kicked open the double doors of the police station.

Bennett, who was covering a night shift for a cop whose kid was playing in his first high-school football game, looked up from the work on his desk and called out, "Hey, you, that's enough of that, wise guy."

Mick looked over at Bennett and extended his middle finger. Laughing loudly, he led his two saviors out to the street.

"So you two got a score to settle with the big-shot cop, too, huh? That's just fine."

Kruger's brothers-in-law nodded. "Damn straight, Mick," said Carl, the shorter one. "We're gonna bust his ass."

His taller brother, Eddie, agreed eagerly. "Oh, yeah, I'm gonna rip him good. You wait and see."

"We ain't waitin' a fuckin' second," Mick growled. "You know where he's stayin'?"

"You bet," Carl told him. "We been gettin' it all fixed out. We're gonna ram that bastard's ass."

Mick grinned. "So what are we waitin' for, my men? Let's roll it."

Eddie pointed to the jeep that was parked in front of the station.

Mick slapped their shoulders and ran to it, snickering and hooting. The brothers followed.

Harry closed the door as quietly as he could and dug into his jacket pocket for his car keys. He had to walk past the house's tiny adjoining garage in order to reach his car. He hadn't paid much attention to it when he arrived but he glanced over to it now. He'd never seen Jenny driving a car and was half curious to see if she owned one.

The garage door was a little more than halfway up. It made for a very heavily shadowed interior. And the night was a particularly dark one. A storm looked to be on the way. Clouds were drifting in and blocking the starlight.

Even so, Harry could see well enough to make out the small car's rear end. It was a gray Oldsmobile Firenza. He could read its license-plate number: 1AQ175.

Harry looked back at the house.

A bright red Datsun 280ZX glided to a stop in front of La Bahía Hotel. A beaming Inspector Horace King bopped out of the car. He reached into the rear of the car and withdrew a magnum of Taittinger champagne. The sight of the bottle brought a whistle to his lips. He looked up at a window on the second floor. He reached back into the car and took out a small suitcase and a green canvas slipcase with a handle. The case contained his Smith and Wesson 3000 shotgun.

Still whistling, he shifted his gear to one arm so that he could lock his car, then jauntily sauntered into the hotel.

He was still whistling when he hit the second floor. Checking door numbers, he made his way to Harry's and knocked.

"Callahan. Wake up, mother. The heat is off. It's celebration time, Harry. Your bad white ass is cooled out. So drop those trousers and let that honky moon of yours shine at the world."

When Harry didn't respond, Horace knocked again. "Open up, Harry. So says Horace the—"

The door suddenly flew open and Horace found himself staring at two brute-faced thugs and a grinning psycho-looking son of a bitch.

Horace knew it was bad.

The thugs were pointing handguns at his head. He didn't move a muscle or say a word.

Just like friggin' Harry to have these scum hanging out in his hotel room.

The big guys pulled him into the room and shut the door behind him.

Horace looked around the room, half expecting to see Harry's body on the floor or pieces of it anyway. He was slightly relieved when he saw nothing. He hadn't really thought it possible. Harry was just too damned mean for these three cretins to take out. But, then, there was always the chance. You never really know, do you?

Horace eyed the three men. Should he know now?

Horace wasn't worried yet and he certainly wasn't afraid. Callahan might still pull this out. If it was anybody else . . .

The psycho-looking bastard reached into the back pocket of his jeans and quickly whipped his arm up in front of him.

Horace heard a click and then saw a gleaming eight-inch blade flick up out of his clenched fist.

Horace knew.

The knife man sneered. "So long, Sambo."

Horace thought his last thought. Get these bastards, Harry. Get them good.

Harry coasted to a stop in front of Ray Parkins's house. The case had just taken a bizarre and totally unexpected turn. Theories and theorists be damned. What the hell was going on? Why had Jenny Spenser's car been at Ray Parkins's place earlier that night? Why had it been parked up the road and away from the house? And where the hell had Jenny Spenser been? She hadn't been in the car. She hadn't been in the house. Ray and the scum apparently hadn't known anything about her or the car.

Things had just taken a sharp turn and were laying out in a whole different direction.

First Jannings and his weirdness. Then his kid and his strange choice of high-school pals. And now a car, parked in the last place it should be at one point and right back home at another.

Harry wanted answers fast. He wanted background and connections. He wanted it all. Tonight. He'd start with Ray Parkins and work his way through to Jannings and his kid and then Jenny Spenser.

A light was still on in the house. Harry called out as he stepped through the splintered front door. There was no reply. He walked into the parlor and saw Ray lying on the floor twisted into an impossible position. He knew immediately from the rigidity of her limbs that she was dead. He moved close and saw the two head shots. No balls to blow off.

He turned to search for a phone and saw the bullet hole in the wall. He looked down at the floor and saw his own face reflected many times in the shards of broken mirror glass.

He remembered. Damn.

He found a phone on the wall in the kitchen and dialed the San Paulo station. He told the switchboard clerk who he was and that he wanted to report a homicide. He was put on hold for a few seconds and then was surprised to hear Bennett's voice.

"Inspector."

"Bennett, I'm glad you're there. Send somebody out to Ray Parkins's house. She's getting ripe. I'm coming in. I want the punk I brought in earlier and an interrogation room when I get there."

"You can't have him, Inspector."

"Why the hell not?"

"He's gone. A little while ago."

"Who sprung him?"

"Kruger's brothers-in-law."

Harry's face tightened. "Swell."

He was about to hang up when Bennett spoke again. "Listen, Inspector. I've been busy here. But I'm going to run that plate for you now."

"Forget about the plate."

"Okay. If you're sure. I can—"

Harry hung up.

Jenny stood in front of her bedroom dresser. She was fully clothed and wearing her maroon ski jacket. Her shoulder bag lay on the bureau top in front of her. As did six .38-caliber cartridges. She loaded them into her gun. When she finished, she slipped the revolver into her bag and looped the strap over her shoulder.

She reached over to switch off her dresser lamp and caught sight of her reflection in the mirror over the bureau.

She turned away from it quickly and left the house.

"I don't know nothin' and I wouldn't tell you if I did. Now get the hell away and let me go to sleep. I ain't talkin' no more."

With that, Mrs. Kruger slammed down the corrugated-metal gate to the market and left Harry standing near the end of the San Paulo Pier. He hadn't gotten any information from the woman, but he was reasonably sure that her brothers and the punk weren't around. Or, at least, that she had no knowledge of them.

He left the market and crossed the space between it and the next building. A van was parked there illegally. Harry was walking by its front end when a huge fist swung out from behind the side of the van and sank into his gut.

Pain knifed through his midsection and coursed up through his veins to his brain. He tried to fight a doubling-over reflex but was only partially successful. Before he could do anything, a first smashed into his neck below his right ear and another one slammed into his left side. He was scissored by the blows and could only drop to his knees.

He knew he had found the brothers.

And he knew he was in a damn bad spot.

He tried to stand and took another horrendous shot to the stomach. He grabbed the arm that had hit him and yanked it in the direction it had come from. A body stumbled by him. He still had one knee on the ground and was trying to raise himself to both feet when he was kicked in the cheekbone. His head snapped back and his body crashed against the van.

He had found the punk.

He reached inside his jacket for the Magnum but before he could grip it, the shorter brother closed on him and pounded his rib cage with alternating lefts and rights. The punches hammered the breath out of his chest and he gasped for air. As he sucked it in his left temple exploded and he felt his face bounce off the surface of the pier.

He forgot the pain and thought only of standing up. If he stayed down, he knew he was dead.

He started to get up when he was kicked in the stomach. The force of it lifted him up and then dropped him to the ground. A surge of acidic bile burned his chest and throat, and gagged him. He was simultaneously choking it down and reaching for the Magnum again when strong hands dragged him to his feet.

They didn't want to kill him too fast.

They wanted to play awhile.

In angry desperation and without aim or tactic, he swung wildly and connected with the taller brother. It was a good shot that caught the scum on the point of the chin. He went down like a felled tree.

But before Harry could grip his weapon, his arms were pinned as the shorter brother bear-hugged him from behind. Harry spun and whirled himself around, trying to shake the slime off his back, but he couldn't. Then his sternum was battered by a crunching, piercing smash that shorted out his consciousness for a second or two. The pain was so intense that it canceled out all the other pain and then itself. For a sudden, beguiling moment he felt almost giddy.

The arms released him and he dropped. The hard wooden mass of the pier smacked him back into full awareness. He saw the faces of the two brothers hanging above him. He groaned loudly and rolled onto his stomach to mask his move for the Magnum. This time he seized hold of its butt and pulled it from the holster. He thought his move was quick but his sense of timing had grown imprecise as the severity of the attack increased.

The Magnum was kicked out of his hand. He saw it hit the surface of the pier and skid away to splash into the ocean.

The punk stood over him now, brandishing a rifle or a riot gun or a shotgun. The weapon seemed familiar. Harry guessed it to be the source of the crushing blow to his chest.

The punk was giggling.

"So, cop, you ain't so smart now, are you? You fuckin' son of a bitch," the punk was shouting. "You're dead, cocksucker, you are *dead*."

He raised the shotgun over his head and screamed, "*Fuckin' cop*." Then he swung it down, butt first, to club Harry. He did it again. And again.

The brothers started to kick.

The force of the clubbing and the kicking bounced Harry to the edge of the pier. He could feel himself bleeding but no longer felt the pain.

Then Mick stopped and signaled the brothers to lift Harry up.

When they had raised his limp body to his knees, Mick chuckled and smashed Harry across the face with the barrel of the shotgun.

Harry's body bucked backward. The brothers let go of him and he crashed through the wooden railing that lined the pier.

Mick and the brothers jumped forward to watch him plunge into the dark water below.

The ocean sucked him down out of sight and gurgled nothing but bubbles to the surface.

Mick and the brothers laughed.

16

Jenny stood before the door of a large white Victorian house just north of the center of town. The neighborhood had been San Paulo's finest during the twenties and thirties. It was still very good through the forties and fifties. The sixties and seventies brought change, however, though not decline exactly. Now "revival" and "restoration" were the key words on Victor Street. This particular house was flawlessly and impeccably well kept.

Jenny had tried the back door, the rear windows, and the garage. Everything was locked up tight. She wanted this one done, and done quickly. She had heard a voice at Ray's house that had made her shiver. She had not planned on that one being in San Paulo. He had been a loose end, to be researched and sought out, and then, later, in whatever place, destroyed. Him above all.

But this one she wanted very much, to be finished this night. Before a new morning light. This one was, perhaps, minutely different from the others. But only in intent, not in deed. And for Jenny now, and certainly for Elizabeth forever, only the deed, the action, the committed crime, mattered.

Before returning to her car to sit and wait for opportunity, Jenny, on sheer whim, on a fugitive impulse, reached out and tried the front door.

It was not locked.

She refused to consider implications or possibilities. Only facts were important. The door was open. The one she sought was inside the house. So be it.

She went in.

Jenny looked around at the spotless, museumlike rooms. The vestibule doors were opened to a parlor that was crowded with couches, easy chairs, end tables, picture frames, knick-knacks, and mementos. The personal history of generations was displayed in the room. The setting might well have been unchanged for decades. Jenny was here tonight to alter that history and to mar that setting. She would change them, eternally and indelibly, as she and her sister had been changed.

She closed the front door softly behind her and walked through the vestibule and across the large parlor. She came to a small triple-connecting hallway. She guessed that directly in front of her would be the kitchen and back-porch area. To one side she could see a formal dining room. On the other side a sturdy oak door closed off what she assumed would be the living room or study.

She drew her weapon from her bag and held it out in front of her with one hand as she carefully and slowly opened the heavy door with the other.

A pastel-shaded Tiffany lamp on an ornately hand-carved wooden table cast a soft, diffuse glow about the room. Books lined the walls, filling ceiling-high bookcases. Stuffed game birds and silk-flower arrangements embellished each corner of the room. Official-looking photographs and documents dotted the walls and yellowed with age inside elaborate, decorous frames. A large, handsome desk dominated the space. A small couch and two stuffed velour-covered parlor chairs faced it from a short distance away.

Jenny entered the room. She raised the gun in front of her.

Someone was sitting in one of the chairs. A man. His back was to her and only his head was visible above it.

She stared at the back of that head, with its close-cropped, neatly combed brown hair and its long, slender neck.

She could picture well the soft, delicate features of its head. The thin nose. The anxious eyes. The indecisive lips. The weak, almost feminine chin. The prominent Adam's apple below it.

She could see the face well.

Floating above her, backed by a black sky, taut with fear, the head quivering in near-rabid nervousness. The cheeks glistening with the sweat of panic and dread.

She could hear a voice. Not the face's voice but another— the one she had heard earlier. The one that made her shiver.

"*Stick* it, Alby."

It taunted. Ridiculed. Incited.

"What are you, queer? *Do* it, faggot. *Do* it."

Jenny could remember the sound of the slap. The one blow that had not been directed at her or Elizabeth.

The face jerked forward.

It cringed in upon itself and started to sob.

The face wet her face as it dripped tears of its own to mingle with hers.

But still it acted. Its head bobbed forward as its narrow body pushed and invaded.

Jenny brought her other hand up to grip the gun. A finger

squeezed the trigger gently. Another pressed down on the hammer.

She circled around to the front of the chair.

Sitting before her, in pajamas and a robe, under a blanket, was a cadaverous young man who did nothing to acknowledge her presence. He did not move, speak, or blink. Jenny looked down at his slippered feet and saw a long plastic tube that led under the chair on which he sat. The tube was filled with yellow liquid.

She lowered her gun as she understood.

"Drop it."

The voice came from the doorway. It was a grim, defeated sound.

Jenny looked over to see Alby's father, Police Chief Jannings, pointing a revolver at her. She let go of her weapon. It thudded dully to the carpet.

She looked back at Alby.

"He couldn't live with it," Jannings said, and crossed the room to stand by her, in front of his insentient son. "The other vermin didn't care. But the guilt was like an acid in his gut. It ate at him. Turned his mind." He looked at her. "He actually wanted you to come back. To revenge yourself on him. He used to sit up nights, waiting, praying for you to come. One night he couldn't wait any longer. He drove off the road and slammed himself into the retaining wall. Alby never did a lot of things the right way. He didn't do that right, either. He lived. If you can call this life."

He lowered his gun. "Now you're here. And he doesn't even know it."

The speech had been a long time coming for Jannings. Now that he had begun, it was time to complete the confession. The burden had been borne too long. He was tired.

These things were coming to their end. Let them all be finished.

"It was my fault. I should have let him be punished then . . . with the other . . . filth. But, no, he was my boy, my only child." Jannings stepped close to the inert figure in the chair and gently stroked his forehead and hair.

"His mother died giving birth to him. So he was twice special to me. He was all of her I had left."

Jenny tried not to listen to the words. They could weaken purpose. Destroy intent. She tried to shut them out, but still they seeped through her defense.

Jannings went on. "I was a public figure. I was afraid. For him. And for me. So I did things. I . . . fixed it."

He looked at Jenny with beaten, sad eyes.

"Go. Let it be over."

No. Jenny's heart raced. Her mind and memory screamed. *No.*

"There's one left," she said in a firm, resolute voice.

"Leave that evil slime to me. He's in my jail right now." Jannings was coming alive with anger. "He's the only one who found out what I did. He preyed on Alby. Corrupted him. He's been preying on me ever since. That, too, must end."

"That so, Lester, boy?"

The voice. Jenny turned quickly to the doorway. He was there. Flanked by two bigger men.

Him.

"Make way, sheepfuckers. I'm first. Lemme show you how a man does it."

The words came back to her from the past.

"*Spread,* bitch. Open up."

The words and their pain. And the pain of the beating that began then.

The pain of having him near her, touching her.

"Been waitin' for this, huh, college girl? Don't worry, honey. You ain't gonna be disappointed."

The pain of the humiliation and the torture.

She remembered it all. And the lie, too.

"Let go of the piece, Lester." When Jannings did not move, Mick hurried behind Alby's chair and pressed the barrel of the shotgun against the son's head. "Drop it or we'll splatter what's left of the retard's brains all over the floor."

Jannings released his gun and it fell to the carpet beside him.

Mick smiled, and stepped to Jenny's side. Leaning his face close to hers, he whispered in a raspy voice, "Hi, babe."

The ocean beneath and beside the San Paulo Pier was roughing up. The swells were reaching higher all the time. Each cross-currented collision of waves stretching to or flowing back from the shore brought choppier and foamier crests. The surf ran farther and farther up the beach and the whoosh of the curling, swirling waves grew louder and louder as they crashed on the sand.

An object broke the surface of the steadily churning sea under the pier. It bobbed on the water, narrowly avoiding the numerous underpinnings of the structure.

It was a head.

As it drifted in toward the beach, shoulders and a chest became visible. These soon became a man when he staggered out of the surf.

Battered and bloodied, he clung to an upright wooden support as he gained his balance and caught his breath. When he had gathered sufficient strength, he made his faltering way across the sand.

"You almost fucked up here, Lester," Mick jeered at the police chief. "But, hey, don't worry about it. I'm gonna take care of every little thing and the best part is, you don't have to do a damn thing but sit on your fat ass.''

He picked up Jenny's gun, then looped an arm around her shoulders. ''But first, me and the little honey gonna relive us some good old times.'' He pushed Jenny at the shorter brother. ''You bring her along, Carl. Let's *go*.''

Jenny stumbled against the man, who grabbed her under her arm to keep her from falling. He squeezed tightly and shoved her toward the doorway.

She did not resist but looked back at Jannings. Mick and the other brother started toward the doorway, too.

As soon as they turned their backs to him Jenny saw Jannings jump for his gun. Carl, the man who held her, yelled a warning.

Mick swung around and shot Jennings with her gun. He toppled to the floor. Mick ran over to the body, smiled, and cocked the gun.

''*Jesus*, Mick,'' Carl called to him. ''You didn't say nothin' about doin' the chief.''

Mick giggled. ''Don't sweat it. It's a freebie. We just sign our little honey's name to it.''

He aimed and fired at Jannings's crotch.

''Let's *move*,'' he yelled, and ran from the room. The brothers, shoving Jenny forward, followed him.

When they had gone, Alby, impassive and silent, sat alone beside the body of his dead father.

The door to room 213 in La Bahía Hotel burst open. Harry Callahan, dripping seawater and blood, filled the threshold. In the spill of streetlight falling through the room's windows, Harry looked down to see a fallen Pissface. His head was bloodied but he still breathed.

Harry stepped into the room and saw Horace lying in a

pool of dark, congealed blood. Two mouths gaped up at him. Horace's throat had been cut.

Harry's eyes glazed over.

He went to the room's cheap dresser and pulled open its bottom drawer. He took out a rectangular mahogany case and opened it.

Inside was the gleaming Magnum automatic.

He lifted the awesome weapon out of its felt niche and picked up a full ammunition clip from the box.

He rammed the clip into place.

Mick hurled Jenny to the sand. The brothers smirked as he laid the shotgun down.

They were under the boardwalk. In the same spot.

"If there's any left," he said, grinning, "you boys can have a piece."

Jenny watched them leer and slap one another's backs. He wants it to happen all over again, Jenny realized, because of the lie. Well, this time, she swore to herself, it would not be.

She scurried to her feet and faced Mick.

His eyes widened. "I wonder if it's any better after all these years."

He started to laugh as he unbuckled his belt.

Jenny crouched, her arms spread in front of her. "Okay, you prickless scum," she said in a strong, firm voice, "you want to try again? Think maybe you can get it up this time? Think you can maybe get it to work?"

Mirth flashed out of Mick's face. The brothers looked at each other.

"You want me, you putrid little maggot?" Jenny yelled at him. "You come and get me. This time you'll have to rape my dead body."

Mick's eyes bulged. He growled a long, rasping roar that ended in a manic bellow and charged her.

Jenny held her ground until he was nearly upon her, then swung her foot out with all the power and flex her body could summon.

She felt the back of her toes and the top of her foot drive up into his testicles. She could feel them squish and flatten.

Mick was lifted off his feet and seemed to hang in midair before dropping to his face on the sand. He clutched his groin with both hands and screamed with pain and rage.

The brothers recovered from their own shock and advanced on her. Mick wildly waved them back.

"*No. No.* The bitch is *mine*," he screamed from his curled-up position. "*Mine.*"

Jenny sneered down at him. "Think you're man enough this time?"

Mick shrieked with outrage and leaped at her. He drove his shoulder into her stomach in a tackle that knocked her off her feet and bounced her off a boardwalk support piling.

She crumpled to the sand beneath him but instantly drove her tensed, extended fingers into his face, hoping to spear his eyes. Missing them, she slashed the fingernails of both hands across his cheeks.

Mick yelped with pain but swung out and smashed the side of her head with an open hand. Her cheekbone and temple sizzled with white-hot pain.

Mick then backhanded her viciously and gripped her throat with viselike fingers. Jenny gagged and tried to jab at his eyes and face, but he stretched backward so that she could not reach him.

She thought the immense pressure of his fingers would pierce the flesh of her neck and throat. She was choking.

Her hands flailed out as she hoped to push off the ground

and roll out from under him, but she could not secure a hold that would give her the necessary leverage. He understood immediately and jammed a knee between her breasts to press her hard to the sand.

Jenny's arms flailed even more desperately now as she struggled to twist around and out of his grip. Her effort to roll away was in vain, but her fingers brushed against a length of driftwood. She strained to edge it into her grasp and felt what seemed to be nails sticking out of one end of it.

When she finally held it firmly, she thrust its jagged end into Mick's face.

He howled. And flipped back off her, seizing his face.

When Jenny saw the brothers rush to his aid, she jumped to her feet and ran out from under the boardwalk.

"She's splittin', Mick," a confused Eddie told him.

Mick rolled in the sand, yowling. "*Get* her. Get the bitch."

Jenny climbed up to the boardwalk and ran toward the arcade area and Beach Street beyond it. The brothers, close behind her, jumped onto the boardwalk and gave chase. Mick stumbled as he rose, furiously wiping the blood from his eyes. When he could see again, he grabbed the shotgun and followed.

When he reached the boardwalk and saw the brothers chasing Jenny, he yelled to them with desperate rage, "*Get* the bitch."

Jenny flung her arms out in front of her as she ran, pumping the air frantically for momentum and speed. She could hear the heavy footsteps of her pursuers. They were gaining on her.

The game stands and concession booths blocked her path to the street. Her original instinct was to run to the street and scream for attention and people. She knew that Callahan lived in La Bahía, and she was sure that if she could make it that far, he would respond to her shouts even if no one else did. And he was enough.

She gambled a few seconds of slowdown and looked over her shoulder. The brothers were closer than she thought. They moved fast for such bulky men. She knew she would have to change her plan now if she was going to survive. She could not waste precious seconds weaving through the maze of kiddie rides that fronted the arcade. Even if she cleared them before the brothers caught up with her, she would still have to scale the gate that was locked each night to section off the amusement area from the sidewalk and street.

There was no hope that way.

She needed noise and the time to create it.

She grabbed her jacket pocket and felt her keys inside it. She reached inside and clutched them tightly.

She veered away from the arcade and ran, with the widest, quickest stride possible, toward the carousel house.

She reached the carousel and spent breathless, maddening seconds unlocking the doors. She then rushed inside, slapped the glass doors closed, and locked herself in.

The brothers flung themselves onto the doors and pushed. Jenny faced them, less than six inches away, the flimsy glass her only, momentary protection. The brothers' breath fogged the doors as they pulled and pushed against the lock.

She looked beyond them and saw Mick running toward them.

Jenny turned and ran to the center of the carousel's turntable. She quickly switched it on and shifted into gear. The starter bell rang a short warning and the carousel began to move as gay, childlike calliope music played accompaniment.

She looked back at the door. Mick's bleeding, mauled face was stretched taut with infuriated frustration. His eyes blazed hate at her. He raised the shotgun and smashed out the glass of the door.

Followed by the brothers, he jumped into the carousel house.

Jenny leaped onto the turntable and ran among the creatures for refuge.

Mick stationed Eddie at the broken doors and sent Carl around one side of the revolving turntable while he advanced in the other direction.

Jenny bent down and slipped under a bounding tiger. The carousel went round and round.

Mick and Carl jumped on and methodically made their way through the sculpted animals.

Jenny saw legs approaching her and scurried beneath a lunging wolf.

Another set of legs walked her way. She scrambled past them, underneath a lion and around a camel.

The turntable passed Eddie and he saw her. He hollered to the others, who turned and headed in Jenny's direction.

She scrambled ahead but stopped suddenly when man legs appeared next to her. She crouched, silent and motionless, until the platform completed another full revolution and Eddie spotted her again. She bolted away from the legs but not quickly enough. Carl grabbed her by the hair and pulled her up. He swung at her face but she turned quickly so that his open-handed blow just grazed the back of her head. She kicked out at his crotch and as he shuffled to the side to avoid her, she pushed.

He released her as he fell backward against a giraffe and ricocheted off it and the platform to bounce against the curving wall of the carousel house.

He cursed at her in pain and anger but got quickly to his feet and waited for her to appear on the next turn around.

Jenny did not have to see him to know that this would be his plan. When she was rounding the back of the house, she jumped off.

She was boxed in. Trapped.

She looked down and saw the restoration supplies. She snatched up a full, heavy paint can and hurled it through a section of the glass wall.

Jenny covered her eyes with her arms as broken glass sprayed everywhere, then she jumped through the shattered wall.

Mick called to the others and sped after her.

Jenny ran out into the amusement area and the Whip, the Haunted House, and the Whirling Dervish blocked her escape to the street. She shifted direction and ran under the roller coaster, which sided and towered over the carousel house.

She pumped her arms and stretched her stride and heaved for breath. She wanted to get under the coaster and lose herself in its labyrinth of supports and struts.

But before she could gain its shelter, she was smashed to the ground by a bone-jarring tackle. She was flipped over roughly, and looked up to see Mick's deranged face hovering over her.

He raised his hand over his head, closed his fist, and threw it down into her face. An involuntary sigh escaped her lips as her head whipped backward.

He punched her again and yanked her to her feet. The brothers arrived and seized her arms. Jenny struggled fiercely against their hold. Mick punched her again to still her. Although each blow had been devastatingly powerful, she was determined not to surrender to the pain and not to lose consciousness.

Mick dug his fingers into her cheeks and squeezed hard. Strangely, the new, pinching hurt cleared her head to full awareness. She looked at Mick. He was giggling now and leaning very close to her.

She spat in his face.

He punched her again and was lifting the shotgun to club her when Eddie spoke.

"Holy shit," he said softly, his eyes bugging out as he focused on something.

Mick stopped the clubbing action and looked at Eddie, who was staring straight ahead. He looked at Carl and Jenny, and found them staring, too. He turned around.

A short distance away, silhouetted against a brightly painted concession booth, stood a dripping, bleeding Harry Callahan.

He did not sway or waver but stood still and straight up, the Magnum automatic in his right hand and his right arm at his side.

Jenny saw shock, then fear, and finally rage flicker across Mick's face.

The brothers released Jenny and stepped out to either side and drew their weapons. Mick stepped behind her and slung his arm tight around her throat.

Harry faced them down.

He recognized the shotgun.

Mick moved first. He fired at Harry and blasted the concession booth beside him into splinters. Eddie fired but missed as Harry dropped to one knee, brought his gun arm up in front of him, and fired. The slug blew Eddie up into the air, and his lifeless body somersaulted against the cross-hatched wooden supports of the roller coaster. Eddie slumped to the ground.

Carl fired and then jumped behind a metal sign that listed the standard operating rules for the ride.

Harry dropped and rolled away from the shot.

Mick pumped the shotgun, fired a careless blast at the

rolling figure, and, dragging Jenny along with him, retreated into the cover of the roller coaster's entry house.

The shotgun blast and the pistol shot splintered the boardwalk next to Harry. Carl leaned out from the metal sign to shoot again but popped back behind it when he saw Harry roll up onto his feet.

Harry stood, extended his arm, and fired at the sign.

His bullet pierced the metal with a sharp *ping* and blew away the top of Carl's head. The body flopped to the boardwalk.

Harry went after Mick.

He entered the coaster house and looked out of the tunnel to see Mick dragging Jenny onto the track. He followed them as they passed out of his sight.

When he reached the outside of the house and tunnel, Harry spotted Mick climbing to the highest part of the tracks while pushing Jenny up ahead of him.

Harry walked out onto the first level of track and called up to Mick, "Let the girl go, punk."

Mick pushed Jenny up onto the highest section of the roller coaster, climbed up himself, and stood behind her as he pulled her to her feet. He looked down at Harry and laughed. Then he pressed the barrel of the shotgun up under her jaw.

Harry lowered the Magnum automatic to his side.

"I can't do that, cop," Mick shouted. "She's my honey. My prize. We're gonna have ourselves a little reunion. We're gonna have fun."

He laughed some more and shoved the gun tighter to Jenny's throat.

"But it's a hell of an idea, ain't it, cop? Just you and me. That would be something else, huh?"

Harry stared up at him and muttered to himself, "Go ahead, make my day."

Mick glared down at him.

Their eyes met.

Mick swung the shotgun around at Harry, but Jenny threw an elbow at his chin and dropped to the rails as he pulled the trigger.

Harry raised his arm and fired.

The two shots were almost simultaneous.

Mick's missed.

Harry's caught him in the chest and hammered him against the coaster railing.

Harry fired again and took Mick in the head. The bullet sent him crashing through the railing, then he plunged off the track and smashed through the glass roof of the carousel house.

Harry stepped to the edge of the track and looked down. The carousel was still turning. The music was still playing. But only one person rode it. Mick straddled the unicorn, impaled on its horn. He went round and round. His blood striped the white creature's neck bright red.

17

Dawn was a warm glow behind the mountains that rimmed San Paulo's inland side. Yet, even so, the sky above the ocean was beginning to fade from black to light blue. The storm that had threatened the night before had vanished. The clouds had dissolved. The sea was smooth. A thin fog slowly drifted to shore.

Policemen, paramedics, a coroner's examiner, and a photographer worked at their jobs. A few early-morning beach scavengers, armed with their metal detectors, gawked from behind the official crime-scene barriers.

Harry and Jenny stood off by themselves.

He knew now. She had told him all of it.

Jenny watched the dark surface of the water grow lighter and lighter as the sun began to rise behind the town.

Harry watched her.

"What happens now?" she asked.

He did not have a ready answer.

She turned to confront his silence. "Do you read me my rights?"

He still had no answer.

"My rights," she said. "Is that what this is about? Just what are my rights? And why should they be protected now? Where was this concern when I was being beaten and gang-raped? What were my sister's rights when she was tortured and brutalized? And what about justice? Was it justice that they should all just walk away? You don't understand what it's like, Callahan. You never will. No man can."

She turned away from him and stared out at the ocean. "Let's get it over with," she said.

"Inspector . . ."

Harry looked over to see Bennett approaching.

"We found a snub thirty-eight in his belt."

Harry looked at the back of Jenny's head.

"Run it through ballistics," he told the young officer. "I'm sure you'll find it's the murder weapon."

Bennett looked back at the carousel. Mick's body was being hoisted off the unicorn's horn. "Then it's over?" he asked hopefully.

Jenny turned around.

"Yeah," Harry said. "It's over."

Bennett's entire face smiled. His eyes rolled up as he sighed relief to the heavens and left them.

Harry and Jenny stood together a moment, silently watching each other. Then Harry led her away from the boardwalk and the ocean.

A gold-red dawn rose over San Paulo and its people, its carousel, boardwalk, roller coaster, and beach.

A resplendent yellow sun shone hot light and started to burn away the fog.

Mystery & Suspense by GREGORY MCDONALD

__FLETCH AND THE MAN WHO

(B30-303, $2.95, U.S.A.)
(B30-868, $3.75, Canada)

America's favorite newshound has a bone to pick with a most elusive mass murderer! From the bestselling author of FLETCH'S MOXIE and FLETCH AND THE WIDOW BRADLEY.

__FLETCH AND THE WIDOW BRADLEY
by Gregory Mcdonald   (B90-922, $2.95)

Fletch has got *some* trouble! Body trouble: with an executive dead in Switzerland. His ashes shipped home prove it. Or do they? Job trouble: When Fletch's career is ruined for the mistake no reporter should make. Woman trouble: with a wily widow and her suspect sister-in-law. From Alaska to Mexico, Fletch the laid-back muckraker covers it all!

__FLETCH'S MOXIE
by Gregory Mcdonald   (B90-923, $2.95)

Fletch has got plenty of Moxie. And she's just beautiful. Moxie's a hot movie star. She's got a dad who's one of the roaring legends of Hollywood. She's dead center in a case that begins with a sensational on-camera murder and explodes in race riots and police raids. Most of all, she's got problems. Because she's the number one suspect!

MYSTERY . . . SUSPENSE . . . ESPIONAGE

_THE GOLD CREW
*by Thomas N. Scortia
& Frank M. Robinson*   (B83-522, $2.95)

The most dangerous test the world has ever known is now taking place aboard the mammoth nuclear sub *Alaska.* Human beings, unpredictable in moments of crisis, are being put under the ultimate stress. On patrol, out of contact with the outside world, the crew is deliberately being led to believe that the U.S.S.R. has attacked the U.S.A. Will the crew follow standing orders and fire the *Alaska's* missiles in retaliation? Now the fate of the world depends on what's going on in the minds of the men of THE GOLD CREW.

_THE PARK IS MINE
by Stephen Peters   (B30-035, $2.95)

At night, New York's Central Park is a jungle of terrors, both imagined and real. Now, in an act of incredible daring, a lone, angry shadow—his formidable skills of war honed in another jungle thousands of miles away—has transformed the Park into a bloody free-fire zone.

_THE BRINK
by Daniel V. Gallery   (B32-008, $2.25)

A chilling novel about an accident aboard a Polaris sub which threatens to start World War III. "Read it and quake."   *—Bestsellers*

The Best of Adventure
by RAMSEY THORNE

5 EXCITING ADVENTURE SERIES
MEN OF ACTION BOOKS

___**NINJA MASTER**
by Wade Barker
Committed to avenging injustice, Brett Wallace uses the ancient Japanese art of killing as he stalks the evildoers of the world in his mission.
___**#5 BLACK MAGICIAN**   (C30-178, $1.95)
___**#7 SKIN SWINDLE**   (C30-227, $1.95)
___**#8 ONLY THE GOOD DIE**   (C30-239, $2.25, U.S.A.)
                                   (C30-695, $2.95, Canada)

___**THE HOOK**
by Brad Latham
Gentleman detective, boxing legend, man-about-town, The Hook crossed 1930's America and Europe in pursuit of perpetrators of insurance fraud.
___**#1 THE GILDED CANARY**   (C90-882, $1.95)
___**#2 SIGHT UNSEEN**   (C90-841, $1.95)
___**#5 CORPSES IN THE CELLAR**   (C90-985, $1.95)

___**S-COM**
by Steve White
High adventure with the most effective and notorious band of military mercenaries the world has known—four men and one woman with a perfect track record.
___**#3 THE BATTLE IN BOTSWANA**   (C30-134, $1.95)
___**#5 KING OF KINGSTON**   (C30-133, $1.95)

___**BEN SLAYTON: T-MAN**
by Buck Sanders
Based on actual experiences, America's most secret law-enforcement agent—the troubleshooter of the Treasury Department—combats the enemies of national security.
___**#1 A CLEAR AND PRESENT DANGER**   (C36-020, $1.95)
___**#2 STAR OF EGYPT**   (C30-017, $1.95)
___**#3 THE TRAIL OF THE TWISTED CROSS**   (C30-131, $1.95)
___**#5 BAYOU BRIGADE**   (C30-200, $1.95)

___**BOXER UNIT—OSS**
by Ned Cort
The elite 4-man commando unit of the Office of Strategic Studies whose dare-devil missions during World War II place them in the vanguard of the action.
___**#3 OPERATION COUNTER-SCORCH**   (C30-128, $1.95)
___**#4 TARGET NORWAY**   (C30-121, $1.95)

"THE KING OF THE WESTERN NOVEL" IS MAX BRAND

___BROTHERS ON THE TRAIL	(C90-302, $1.95)
___GUNMAN'S GOLD	(C90-619, $1.95)
___HAPPY VALLEY	(C90-304, $1.75)
___LUCKY LARRIBEE	(C94-456, $1.75)
___RETURN OF THE RANCHER	(C90-309, $1.95)
___RUSTLERS OF BEACON CREEK	(C30-271, $1.95)
___FLAMING IRONS	(C30-260, $1.95)
___BULL HUNTER	(C30-231, $1.95)
___RIDER OF THE HIGH HILL	(C30-607, $1.95)
___MISTRAL	(C90-316, $1.95)
___THE SHERIFF RIDES	(C90-310, $1.95)
___SILVERTIP'S CHASE	(C98-048, $1.50)
___SILVERTIP'S ROUNDUP	(C90-318, $1.95)
___SILVERTIP'S STRIKE	(C98-096, $1.50)
___SLOW JOE	(C90-311, $1.95)
___THE STRANGER	(C94-508, $1.75)
___TAMER OF THE WILD	(C94-334, $1.75)
___WAR PARTY	(88-933, $1.50)

CRISIS AVERSION TEAM

__C.A.T. Series#3: CULT OF THE DAMNED

by Spike Andrews (C30-183, $2.25, U.S.A.)
(C30-694, $2.95, Canada)

The city sizzles in an angry heat wave that provokes a crime wave of insane proportions. A rooftop sniper lashes out in exploding lead. A twisted killer leaves a trail of murdered models. And rival Arab overlords take their war to the scorching streets of New York. Now it's up to the special corps of super-elite cops to uncover the link between these seemingly random crimes.

To order, use the coupon below. If you prefer to use your own stationery, please include complete title as well as book number and price. Allow 4 weeks for delivery.